To Save A Mate
:Somewhere, TX

VonBrandt Family

Krystal Shannan

To Save A Mate: Somewhere, TX
VonBrandt Family
Copyright © 2014 KS Publishing
ISBN: 1503014118
ISBN-13: 978-1503014114

All rights reserved.
This book is a work of fiction and any resemblance to persons – living or dead –or places, events, or locales is purely accidental. The characters are reproductions of the author's imagination and used fictitiously. This book contains content that is not suitable for readers 17 and under.

Cover designs by Erin Hill, www.edhgraphics.blogspot.com

All rights reserved.
Please be aware that this book cannot be reproduced, scanned, or distributed in any printed or electronic form without written permission from the author, Krystal Shannan, at krystalshannan@yahoo.com, or within the sharing guidelines at a legitimate library or bookseller. Please do not participate in or encourage piracy of copyrighted materials in violation of the author's rights. Purchase only authorized editions.

WARNING: The unauthorized reproduction, sharing, or distribution of this copyrighted work is illegal. Criminal copyright infringement, including infringement without monetary gain, is investigated by the FBI (http://www.fbi.gov/ipr/) and is punishable by up to five years in a federal prison and a fine of $250,000.

DEDICATION

To my Chick Tale Gals, KC Klein, Jodi Vaughn, R.L Syme, and Lavender Daye. To infinity and beyond!

August, 2014

Somewhere, Texas

CHAPTER ONE

He'd miscalculated the time and was running late. His wolf paced restlessly within, anxious to get out and run with the pack.

Luke glanced across the intersection. The single light atop the pole across the street flickered on in the fading light, its sensor detecting the fading light as the sun set. . He didn't have long to get his ass out to the ranch before the last bit of light disappeared and the moon rose. Once that happened, he wouldn't be driving anywhere until morning.

He gunned the Vortec 6.0L V8 engine and his pickup blew down College Street with a roar. It was a Monday night and the town roads were abandoned. Most of the students from out of town wouldn't start arriving until Wednesday or Thursday for orientation. Somewhere, Texas would really come alive then. The start of a new school year always breathed life into the otherwise boring small town.

Leaning forward, he rolled the dial on his radio, searching for the local country station. The new Brent Kane song, Loved Walked In, blared out from the speakers. Somewhere's very own country rock star stayed over at the Double D ranch north of town whenever he wasn't on tour.

Luke rolled down the window, enjoying the unusually cool breeze.

Movement on the right side of the street caught his eye. One second the road was clear, and the next his headlights highlighted a familiar female figure in the failing light. *No!* His foot slammed the breaks, but the three and a half ton truck just couldn't stop that fast. She disappeared from view and the sickening *thump* that followed made his heart stop and his stomach climb into his throat.

Throwing the truck into park, he leapt out and bent to look beneath his vehicle. *Don't be her. Don't be her. Goddess, please don't let it be her.*

It was.

Her body lay twisted at an odd angle underneath his truck. *He'd killed her.*

He sank to the ground next to her, tears watering his eyes. The asphalt bit into his knees like shards of glass. The pain was nothing compared to the fear that he'd lost the only girl he'd ever cared about. It didn't matter that she thought they were just high school classmates. Luke had known since junior high, Kara McClure would eventually be his.

"Kara?"

He touched her neck, looking for a pulse. It was faint, but the blood pooling beneath her body meant it wouldn't last long. "Fuck. You can't die on me, Kara. Do you hear me?" Leaning forward, he ignored basic first aid rules and pulled her out from under the giant truck. He put his face to hers, feeling for breath. The tiniest puff of air blew against his cheek, but even that was labored. He could hear a gurgle in her chest.

She would be dead in minutes. He had no doubt in his mind. There wasn't time to get her to the hospital, or to call for an ambulance. Losing her wasn't an option.

He glanced up at the orange sky, now laced with shades of purple. Time was running out. He would shift as soon as the moon rose. If he didn't take a chance now, he'd lose her forever. Somewhere without Kara wasn't anywhere at all. His life would be over if she died tonight. He lifted her from the asphalt and hugged her to his chest. Warm liquid from her head wound slicked his left hand and tears began to fall down his cheeks.

"Chun tú Geallaim mo chroí agus anam go deo."

No hesitation. The words rolled from his tongue as if he'd been waiting to say them his whole life.

"*Chun tú Geallaim mo chroí agus anam go deo,*" he repeated, pleading from the depths of his being for the spell to take hold quickly, for her blood to stop running in sickening warm streams down his wrist.

The ancient pledge would bind his essence to hers and heal her wounds. She would be able to recover from nearly any injury for as long as he lived. He'd deal with the consequences of his choice later. For now all that mattered was that Kara lived.

"Fight, Kara. Please."

Slowly he felt the pull. The energy that surrounded him shifted, and he growled as pain radiated through him from his head down through his chest. Her injuries were severe, and it would take most of the night for the magick to heal her broken bones and internal injuries. The blood spilling from her head stopped. He gritted his teeth against the pain.

He stood, lifting her in his arms. The streets were still quiet. No one had coming running to see what happened. He laid her out gently on the back seat of his truck, propping up her head with a couple of his old t-shirts. Time was running short. Jumping into the driver's seat, he pulled the shifter out of park and floored the gas pedal.

Fifteen minutes later, he pulled off the highway and turned down the dirt road that cut across all three of the VonBrandt ranches. The road disappeared, and he drove through some tall grass into a grove of pine trees, hiding his truck from view.

Magick shivered and tensed across his skin, warning him the shift was coming. He gave Kara one last look before getting out of the truck. His muscles burned from the coming change, and his body screamed in pain from Kara's injuries. Tonight's run was not going to be a pleasant one.

He stripped out of his clothes and tossed them into the bed of the truck just before the change swept over him, changing him into a sleek black and grey wolf. He wanted to stay and watch over the truck, but his wolf had been raring to run all day in anticipation of the full moon. She would be safe. No one would bother her.

Raising his head to the velvety black sky, he loosed one long howl. A few moments later he heard a chorus of answers from deeper in the hills. He leapt forward into a run, but stumbled and yelped, surprised by the intensity of the pain. He'd thought after shifting it might have faded a little.

No such luck. Standing slowly, he tested his legs again, reminding himself it was phantom pain and not his. A few minutes later he managed to move forward, first at a slow walk and then a faster lope. There would be no hunting for him tonight. It would take all of his concentration just to stay on his feet.

***

Something was terribly wrong. She couldn't remember the last time she felt so much pain. The hardness of the street had disappeared and the cold emptiness that had enveloped her was gone. She could remember air slipping from her lungs, unable to be replenished. Yet now she could draw a full breath. It hurt, but it was possible.

She hadn't planned to jump in front of a truck. But when she'd tripped in the bushes and stumbled out into the middle of the street, the blinding headlights just froze her in place. And she hadn't fought it. At least in death she would be with her parents again. In that split second she'd almost been thankful for the haphazard accident. Though the poor soul who'd hit her must be devastated.

Tears welled in her eyes and ran in streams down her cheeks at the thought of causing someone that kind of grief. It would've been better to die quietly and alone, not involving anyone else. At least then, the pain would have only been hers to bear. God knows her bitchy, backstabbing roommate wouldn't have cared. Neither would her supposed boyfriend, since she'd caught them together at his place. In bed.

Her eyes opened slowly to darkness. The faint smell of hay and horse lingered on the seat where she was sprawled. In fact, the truck smelled like it'd recently been parked in a barn.

Feeling around, she slowly pulled herself into an upright position on the seat and peered out the window at the full moon in the sky above her. Wolves howled not too far off, and she shuddered. The sound had always scared her as a child, even though her dad had always assured her the wolves would never hurt her.

The tears returned in a rush at the memory of her dad. He was gone. So was her mom. They had always gone on vacation in August for their anniversary, but this trip to the spa out in Nacogdoches would be their last. The police officer on the phone earlier today had informed her that a tractor-trailer had lost control on the highway and flipped over, crushing two cars in the process. He tried to soothe her hysterical crying by saying they hadn't suffered, but it didn't help.

They were gone. Forever. The one other person she had in her life, at least the one she thought she could count on, was screwing around with her sorority sister behind her back. She and Vincent had been together for almost five years.

What had she done to deserve such a betrayal?

What was there left to live for? When she'd started running away from Vincent's house, there hadn't been a plan in her mind. Just that she wanted to escape the pain.

She didn't have anyone left in her life that cared.

A cloud moved over the moon and everything fell

into pitch blackness. More howls echoed from the hills ahead of the truck. It sounded like a whole pack. She knew she was safe in the truck, at least for now, but who had hit her, and where were they now? Why had they left her in the truck?

The clouds shifted again and moonlight flooded the field behind the truck. Not much light filtered through the pine tree branches above, and the truck stayed mostly in darkness. She considered getting out and trying to walk, but every time she moved, her body screamed in pain. Eventually it was too much, and she laid back down on the seat and drifted into a restless sleep.

***

Luke approached the truck slowly, wondering if Kara was asleep or awake. It was going to be damn hard to explain why all of his clothes were in the bed of the truck and not on his body.

The pine needles scratched his bare feet. He reached over the side of the bed of the truck and grabbed his jeans and t-shirt, wincing when the belt buckle clanked loudly against the inside wall.

"Hey bro, wanna get some coffee when we get ba—" His brother's voice broke off at the same time two very blue eyes peered through the back window. "Luke, what the hell, dude?" Noah shouted and ducked behind a couple of large pine trees. "Is that why you were so distracted last night during the hunt? I thought dad was gonna chew your ear off for letting go of that deer."

Luke yanked on his pants and pulled the t-shirt on while Kara continued to stare, her gaze flitting between him and the place where his buck naked brother was hiding in the trees. Her eyes were empty, like she'd cried all her emotions out and only the shell of her remained.

"Noah, go back to the house. I'll see you later."

"Yeah, whatever. Mom and dad are gonna eat you for lunch when they hear about this. Don't think I didn't notice that new ink of yours."

"Leave it be, Noah." He yelled, but Noah had already shifted and taken off.

Damn it.

He didn't know what he was going to say to Kara, much less his mom and dad, and that wasn't even the half of it. He stared down at the Celtic markings that wrapped around his wrists. Kara would have identical ones on her wrists as well.

Where to even begin?

He pulled open the back passenger door, expecting a battery of questions, but instead she gave him nothing. Her long, beautiful, strawberry blonde hair was stained with blood from the accident and clumped together in wads. The creamy white skin of her cheeks that he had dreamed of touching was splotchy and red from crying, and her wrinkled clothes were covered in black bits of asphalt and bloodstains.

His gaze narrowed in on her hands. Both were laying lifelessly in her lap, and both of her wrists bore his bond marks. It wasn't really something that could easily be hidden. The bracelets, so-to-speak, were dark green and about three inches wide.

"Kara. I'm so sorry. It was late and I... and I didn't have time to take you anywhere."

She nodded, her gaze staring through him more than at him. He wished she'd say something. Anything would be better than this dead silence. She didn't respond. She just kept staring, her eyes blank and void of any emotion whatsoever.

"I'm gonna take you back to your place, okay?" He knew she was living at the KAS - Kappa Alpha Sigma - sorority house. He'd seen her parents help her move in a few days ago. He and his twin brother lived across the street in AKO -Alpha Kappa Omega - and Noah spent the entire time ribbing him about never asking Kara out.

Vincent Harris was an ass. A great football player, but an ass nonetheless. Luke wasn't the type of guy to rat on someone. Their relationship was their business.

Now it had become his business.

Shit. He was all but married to her in the eyes of his family. They were connected in a way no human couple ever could be. His essence lived inside her now, linking him to her forever. It couldn't be undone. Ever.

He closed the door on her still-silent form, went to the driver's side, and got in. A few minutes later they were rolling down College Street toward Greek row.

The large sorority and frat houses were "old school" plantation style. White. Tall columns in the front. Dozens of windows. They varied a little in shape and size, but not much. If you were new to the campus, the only way you could tell them apart was by the letterhead over the front doors. Even the front lawns were kept perfectly manicured and gorgeous. Shrubbery lined the front of all the houses, and large pine trees were scattered throughout the front and back yards.

Her sorority's house was the last house on the street, on the corner, just across from his fraternity's house. Their houses often had parties together during Greek week and several of his Greek brothers dated KAS girls.

He pulled to a stop by the curb and got out. Kara made no move to exit the truck on her own. He opened the door for her and offered his hand. She laid her small palm in his large one and he noticed her eyes drift to their matching tattoos.

Still, her face remained unchanged and she said nothing. "I can explain." He murmured, tucking her small frame against his large one. She was so cold. And shivering? Maybe it was still just the shock of the accident. "Why don't you get a shower, and I'll go get us some breakfast from Meg's Bakery. I'll be right back." There wasn't much a kolach or two from one of the best bakeries in central Texas couldn't fix. The town actually got tourists, just stopping through to eat at Meg's Bakery. The trip would at least give him a few more minutes to decide what the hell he was going to tell her.

When they got to the front door, Kara pulled a small set of keys from her pocket and fumbled with it a moment before getting the lock to turn. The large white door swung open and a semi-dark foyer lay before them. It was unlikely that anyone was up; it was barely six am. Most of the girls at KAS barely stirred before eight, even once classes started.

"Are you okay to get to your room?"

She pulled away and nodded, moving toward the stairs directly to her left. "I'll be fine," she murmured. "You can leave."

"I'll be back in fifteen with some food, okay. You need to eat something."

No comment. No glance back over her shoulder. She was like a freaking zombie. What had happened to the sweet, carefree, always smiling girl he'd grown up with? The Kara he knew and loved could put a smile on anyone's face. And her voice. Damn, she had the singing voice of an angel.

He pulled the door closed. A jingle caught his ear and he looked back. She'd left her keys in the lock. Pulling them free, he pocketed them and hurried back to his truck. He needed to get back to her as soon as possible, but she deserved a few minutes to clean up and decompress.

***

Kara climbed the stairs slowly. She'd heard the door close and the echo of Luke's footsteps on the wooden porch as he'd walked away from the house. He'd been so kind and comforting, but she barely knew him, and he and his brother were the 'campus bachelors'. Every girl tried to go out with them. Many girls managed to make it happen once, but it was uncommon to get a second date.

Vincent had always made her feel special, like she was the only star in his universe. But seeing him fucking her roommate - in his bed, the bed they'd shared - made her sick. How could he betray her like this? Especially when she needed him so badly right now.

She got to the top of the stairs and walked down the hall to her room. Brushing her fingers across her pocket, she realized she'd left her keys in the door downstairs. But her bedroom door was ajar. *Fuck.*

She pushed it open, and new waves of tears welled up into her swollen eyes. Her roommate Samantha was reading in the chair next to the window.

"Kara," Samantha looked up slowly. Her eyes got big

and she jumped from the chair, dropping her book to the floor. "Oh my God, girl, what happened to you?"

Kara raised her arm. "How could you?" Tears poured down her cheeks in fiery rivers. "You're my roommate. My sorority sister!"

"I don't know what you are talking about, Kara. Calm down. You look like you got hit by a truck."

"I *did*! I tripped and stumbled into the middle of the road after running from Vincent's house last night."

"You were at Vincent's?" Samantha's eyes got wide. She took a step back and nervously twisted a trailing piece of her bleach blonde hair. "When?"

"Just in time to see him eating something he shouldn't have been, bitch. But you go right ahead and keep the lying sonofabitch. I don't want him anymore."

She turned and dashed back out of her room. Taking the stairs two at a time, she burst out the front door and started running across the lawn. But her car wasn't by the curb. She'd left it parked at Vincent's.

Damn it.

"Kara," a familiar male voice called from across the street. She glanced up and saw Noah VonBrandt jogging toward her. At least he had clothes on now. What the hell had he and his brother been doing buck naked out in the forest last night, and why was he suddenly interested in her?

Her body shuddered; the waves of different emotions flowing through her was overwhelming. On one hand she just wanted to curl up in a hole somewhere and die; on the other, she wanted to scream and hit something. Life had served her a pile of crap over the last twenty-four hours, and she'd had just about enough.

Noah was next to her in moments, his strong arms wrapped around her and lifting her from the ground. She stiffened at first, not wanting to be so close to a male body at this point in time, but gave up when his arms only tightened. "I don't know where my idiot of a brother is, but let's get you cleaned up, sweetheart."

Cleaned up? She'd totally forgotten that she was filthy, and her hair felt like it'd been attacked by a superglue bottle. Her hands were covered in scratches and blood stains, too. Then there were these really beautiful but strange tattoos encircling her wrists, pine needle green and permanently inked on her skin. They hadn't been there before the accident. She rubbed her thumb across one of the designs and sighed.

Noah shoved open the front door to the AKO frat house and kicked it closed behind them, barely breaking stride as he carried her up the stairs. "I'm not supposed to be in your room." Kara wiggled a little. Others would see her, and they could get kicked out by their house for breaking rules. Not that guys and girls didn't sneak in all the time to each other's frat houses, but normally it was under the cover of darkness and everyone was drunk off their asses. It certainly was never in the morning when people would be coherent and awake.

"They're passed out. Don't worry. Nobody saw us." He slipped into a room at the end of the hallway and closed the door quietly, locking the bolt at the top before setting her gently on her feet. "Shower is in there. Fresh towels are in the cabinet under the sink. I'll find you something to change into."

She stood, staring at him, unable to understand why he was being so nice. Not that he and his brother were mean. Quite the opposite. She couldn't ever remember a time when Luke and Noah VonBrandt had been anything less than sweet to her when they'd crossed paths. Still. It was strange.

He grabbed a t-shirt and a pair of basketball shorts from a laundry basket full of folded clothes. "They're clean, promise." He pressed them into her arms and turned her toward the bathroom. "This way." He opened the bathroom door and gave her a gentle push toward it. "Do you want me to start the water for you?"

She sniffed and wiped a fresh line of tears from her cheeks. "No, I can do it. I don't know why you are being so nice to me, but thank you."

"You're important to my brother, which makes you important to me."

Important to his brother? Why?

She nodded, not knowing what to say. The bathroom

door closed with a click and she leaned back against it. She was shocked to see an organized, clean bathroom. The mirror was clear of spattered toothpaste, the sink was clean like it'd just been scrubbed. She opened the door under it and pulled out a large fluffy green towel. Laying the towel on the counter, she stripped out of her clothes and stepped into a shower stall cleaner than the one in her room. Kara turned the faucet, and within moments hot water poured over her body. The water around her feet was stained red from the blood caked in her hair.

Hopefully everything would make a little more sense once she was clean.

CHAPTER TWO

Luke parked his truck outside the KAS house, pulling up slowly behind Vincent Harris's pickup truck. *Crap.* He'd never get a chance to talk to her if that jerk was already here. Still, he'd said he would bring her some food, and he wasn't about to turn around and leave without at least checking to make sure Vincent was doing his usual half-ass job of taking care of her.

He hurried up to the front door with the coffee and pastries he'd picked up. Instead of knocking, he used her keys and slipped inside quietly. None of the lights were on in the house, and he could only hear a couple of heartbeats upstairs. Most of the house was empty.

Climbing the stairs, he walked slowly down the hallway toward Kara's door. He paused midway when he heard Vincent and another girl arguing. He heard the girl say "she saw us," and Vincent reply that "he wasn't breaking up with Kara." The unfamiliar girl's heart raced as she wailed that "You promised you were done with

Kara," that "I wouldn't have slept with you if you hadn't."

Luke turned and hurried back out of the house, closing the door softly behind him. Kara wasn't in her room; in fact, she wasn't even in the house. He took a deep breath, trying to get an idea of which way she might've gone. He could scent her, but it was mixed with... Noah?

His boots thunked against the sidewalk as he marched down it and across the street to his frat house, his brother's and Kara's scent growing stronger with each step. What was his trouble-causing, pain-in-the-ass twin brother up to now? At least they weren't identical twins, so it's not like Kara would mistake Noah for him. Still, there was no telling what might come out of Noah's mouth just to make things more difficult.

Hairs on the back of his neck stood up, and a growl rumbled in his throat. If he'd told her anything before he got a chance to explain, he'd beat his brother to a pulp and kick him out of the house. *Whoa, where had that come from?*

He shook his head and took a deep breath. This new possessiveness he felt toward her was going to be tough to curtail if she rejected him. He couldn't force her to like him, but surely she was done with Vincent now if that girl said she'd seen them. Through the years he'd stayed back, in the shadows, just waiting for Vincent to mess up and Kara to leave him. He couldn't stomach being the one to tell her that her beloved boyfriend cheated on her with everything female he could get alone. But he had no problems picking up the pieces and helping her now that she did know the truth. Seeing her so upset and torn apart by Vincent's betrayal was like a kick in the gut. That guy didn't deserve even a "hello" from Kara. And he'd make sure personally, that she was never bothered again.

The AKO house was his home away from home. The guys who lived there were like extra brothers, but they were horny devils, and he didn't trust a single one of them around Kara if they knew she was available. Luckily, most of them were hungover from the couple of cases he and Noah had stocked the kitchen with yesterday, so none of them would notice their absence last night.

Turning into a wolf every month on a full moon was the biggest catch to being one of their kind. They could change whenever else they wanted to, but on a full moon, they were trapped in their wolf bodies until the sun rose that morning. Almost everything else was a perk, except the fact that they had to hide what they were from everyone.

How much would he have to hide from Kara? What would she think if she knew he was a freak of nature, his ancestors cursed by witches a thousand years ago? What the hell was he going to say at all?

He burst into his room and stopped cold, Kara was standing in the bathroom doorway with a brush in her hand. Her wet hair smelled like his shampoo and her floral scent was masked by the piney scent from his bath soap. Goddess alive, he just wanted to go rub his face on her skin and drink in her sweetness. His brother, Noah, was lounging on the recliner in front of their TV, with a look he recognized instantly - adoration.

"Noah." He stalked forward, kicking the corner of the recliner on his way across the room. He set the coffee and bag of pastries on the small table next to Noah, his eyes fixed on Kara.

"Hey, man. Thanks for the coffee."

"Not for you, dude."

Noah laughed. "Yeah, I didn't think so. I'll be downstairs if you need me. Glad you are feeling a little better, Kara." He gave his brother a once over and then cocked his head to the side. "In a bit of a pickle, bro, aren't you?"

"Did you say anything?" Luke hissed.

"Nope, I'll let you figure out that shit."

"What about mom and dad?"

"I wouldn't really do that to you," Noah answered with a grin. "You won't be able to hide those tats for long anyway." He patted him on the shoulder and shook his head before slipping out of the room.

Once his brother had left, Luke trained his gaze back on Kara. The outline of her body showed beneath the white t-shirt, not hiding the swell of her breasts and sweet pink color of her nipples beneath the thin fabric. His brother's long black basketball shorts hung very low on her hips, cinched with a drawstring as tight as she could get them. One of her hipbones peeked above the waistline and he licked his lips, his pants immediately becoming uncomfortably crowded.

Possessive jealousy surged in his blood again. She was his. But in truth, he wasn't any closer to having her than he had been a few days ago. She could choose to reject him. He wouldn't handle it well, but it was her choice. As for Vincent, it would be a cold day in hell before he'd let her go back to him. She deserved someone who truly treasured her. His days of standing aside while that jackass took advantage of her were over.

He walked to his closet and pulled out a lightweight hoodie and brought it to her. "Kara, would you put this on?" Her face colored bright crimson, and she took the hoodie, slipped it on, and zipped it up to her neck. At least he might have a chance to think clearly without having her breasts staring him down from beneath that white t-shirt.

She picked up the brush from the counter from where she'd laid it and began working through her long, wet, red-gold tresses again. "I guess we're even, huh?"

"What do you mean ... oh." He grinned and took a step backward to give her a little more space. "Not quite. I seem to remember flashing a bit more skin."

A tiny smile pulled at the corner of her rose pink lips. Lips he wanted to kiss. They looked petal-soft, and he bet they tasted as sweet as he imagined. She didn't speak again, though. Just watched him intently. He could feel her gaze travel up and down his body before coming to rest on his hands.

He leaned back against the dresser and shoved both hands into his pocket. Some of the bond marks still showed. Noah was right, he wouldn't be able to hide them from his parents for a second. Wearing long sleeves outdoors in this stifling August weather wasn't an option either.

"What do you remember, Kara?"

"I stumbled into the street and got hit by a truck. Was it yours ... you?"

A deep sigh slipped from his chest and his shoulders sagged. "Yes."

"Luke."

"Yeah?"

"I thought I died." She set the brush on the bathroom counter and came into the bedroom, taking a seat on the bean-bag chair in front of the TV. Then she tucked her legs under her chin and hugged them with her arms. Her matching bond marks showed clearly against her creamy white skin.

So small. She'd made herself as tiny as she could; nothing about her body language inviting him anywhere near her.

"You almost did," he finally answered.

"I was covered in blood, but I can't find a wound." She lifted a hand and looked at one of her wrists. "Then there's this."

"Kara, there's an explanation for everything, I just —"

A hard knock at the door interrupted his words. "Luke, dude. Your brother is kicking the shit out of Vincent Harris downstairs. He's yelling about you taking Kara in between the punches."

"Shit." He ran for the door and threw it open, running past his frat brother and down the stairs toward the sound of the ruckus. No doubt Noah would make short work of the varsity football player. For a human, Vincent was a big guy, but he still didn't have a chance against six-foot-five-inches of pissed off werewolf.

***

"Hey, Kara." A red-headed, musclebound guy she'd never met waved at her before following after Luke.

She jumped up from the bean bag and winced. Her body might not have any visible wounds, but her guts told another story. Her insides still felt like they'd been hit by a giant pickup truck, but the pain was better than it'd been earlier. Whatever had healed her was beyond anything modern medicine had at its disposal. But then, what did that mean? How had she been brought back from the brink of death without a scratch?

A loud thump made her pause, but she had to go downstairs. Noah shouldn't be beating up on Vincent for her. But when she saw Vincent's bloody nose and black eye she couldn't help but feel a small amount of satisfaction. Noah had him pinned to the wall with one arm when Luke approached, his fist sailing forward, making contact with Vincent's face with a sickening crunch.

"She's too good for your cheating ass. Get out." Luke's voice rumbled with an authority that made Kara glad it was Vincent they were mad at and not her. *He knows he cheated? How?* She hadn't said anything about seeing Vincent and Samantha together.

The redhead who'd called down Luke down stepped up beside her as she watched Vincent slither out of Noah's grasp and ram him in the stomach. The VonBrandt brother barely made a sound before flipping himself to the side, sending Vincent hurling into Luke, who then swatted him down like a fly. "It's good you're done with that asshole. He's slept with half the girls on the cheer team down in the Sigma Delta Phi 'ho' house."

"Who are you? And how do you know who he's been sleeping with?" *There have been others?*

"Vincent never missed the Delta Phi parties. They're always up for a good fuck, and they buy the best beer." He chuckled. "Luke has been waiting a long time for him to screw up with you."

Waiting? So that means ... He's interested in ... me? Kara watched the way Luke snarled at Vincent before literally tossing him out of the frat house on his ass. If her brain wasn't so screwed up, she might have been able to feel good about Luke and Noah going all ninja protector for her, but as it stood, she was confused and hurt, and really just wanted to crawl into her bed back at her home and disappear.

"Nice tattoos, by the way. When did you and Luke get those?"

"I ... don't remember," Kara murmured, looking down at the markings on her wrists again, and then at Luke, who was powering toward her.

The other guy scurried away, leaving her facing the giant of a man that Luke VonBrandt was. Six-foot-seven-inches, two hundred ten pounds —at least that's what his varsity high school stats had said a couple years ago. He and his brother Noah were the only athletes in Somewhere that were bigger and had better scores than Vincent. It was the only reason she remembered, too. Vincent used to go on and on about how it was unfair that they grew so quickly in high school.

Not that Vincent's six-two was small, but when the

competition was three to five inches taller and outweighed him by thirty or forty pounds, he seemed average by comparison. Vincent was in shape, but he was very slender compared to the VonBrandts, who looked like they might have walked off the set of a gladiator movie.

"Kara, I'm sorry."

"Did he hit Noah first?"

Luke nodded, but his aquamarine blue eyes still held embarrassment and disgust for his actions. "I shouldn't have taken it that far. Neither of us should've."

"I would've kicked him in the nuts," she said, her voice flat. "I think he came out ahead."

A muffled snort of laughter came from Noah a few feet away before he and several other guys sidled out of the room to give Luke and her privacy. What was it with the way they all deferred to him? Maybe he was the house president. That would explain the giant room upstairs. Though his parents' money would explain that as well.

"Can you take me home?" She watched his eyes caress her face and wondered how she could've been so blind not to see his attraction to her before. It'd been so long since Vincent had looked at her that way. She'd forgotten what it felt like to have that... love. It reminded her of the way she would catch her mom or dad looking at her when she would sing to them after dinner.

Something she would never see or get to do again. A tear rolled down her cheek and Luke reached out before she could step back.

He cupped her face in his hand and wiped away the tear with his thumb. She felt safe, but something was off. He'd admitted to hitting her with his truck, almost killing her, and then, what... *she magically woke up like it hadn't happened? And what the hell with the matching tattoos? Who does that to someone without their permission while they are unconscious?*

"Just please take me home." It was all too much right now. If she couldn't be dead, she just wanted to sleep.

"Of course. Do you need to get anything from your room in the KAS house?"

"Just my purse, but I don't need it right now. I just want to lay down." She took a step to the side, breaking contact with his hand. His eyes widened, and his gaze fell to the floor.

"I'll send Noah to get it later. Don't worry about it." He moved back and gestured to the door, not attempting to touch her again.

They left his house, and she climbed into the passenger seat of his truck. He closed the door behind her before jogging around and getting in on his side. The truck roared to life, and within a few minutes he was weaving in and out of her parents' neighborhood like he knew exactly where he was going.

"Why do you know where my house is?"

"I looked it up online. Your parents are listed."

"Oh."

"I promise I'm not a stalker," he said, chuckling and flashing her a quick grin. "Are your parents home?"

"No. They ..." *How do you tell a stranger you just found out your parents were killed?* "They aren't home," she whispered as he pulled up to the curb in front of the home she'd grown up in - a one-story ranch style, yellow brick, cream colored trim, black roof. There were privets growing close to the front wall and around both sides, neatly trimmed and blooming beautifully with tiny white flowers. The Bermuda grass lawn was a little long. *Normally, Dad would probably be mowing it right now, and mom would be in her rocker right by the front door, sipping on a glass of her freshly brewed sweet tea.*

Her vision clouded, and she buried her face in her hands as hot tears poured down her cheeks. This wasn't going to work. She couldn't do this. But she couldn't go back to her room at KAS either. *God, he is just sitting there; probably wishing I would just get out of his truck.*

Without a warning her door opened, and he was pulling her into his arms. *I didn't even hear him get out?* It didn't matter. He was holding her, hugging her. God, she needed a hug. She just wished it was her mom and dad instead of Luke VonBrandt.

"I'm going to take care of you, Kara," he murmured

into her ear as he walked with her to the door. "I need you to tell me how to get in without breaking a window."

She didn't want him to take care of her. She just wanted to be left alone. At the same time, she didn't want to let go of him either. It was a complete brain clusterfuck. Maybe she didn't even know what she wanted.

"The turtle has a key," she said, trying to stifle a sob and tightening her hold around his neck so he could put her legs down.

He complied. She bent to retrieve the turtle from beside her mom's rocker and held out the key. Luke took it, opened the front door and ushered her inside.

Familiar hardwood floors, tan walls, and the smell of leather furniture greeted her senses. The couch and love seat were new, along with the matching recliners. Just another reminder of something her parents had left behind.

She kicked off her canvas sneakers by the door and started walking for the hallway to her right. "You can leave. I'll be fine."

His boots thumped on the floor behind her. *Damn. Just take a hint. I just want to be left alone to cry.* She whirled to face him and sucked in a breath as he halted quickly, but still nearly slammed straight into her. His arms encircled her shoulders to steady her, and she began to shake.

Her voice rose to a high-pitched wail. "Just leave." Tears started gushing again. *Fuck it, just leave me alone.* "Please, go!" She shoved his arms away and slipped into her room, closing the door before he could follow or speak.

CHAPTER THREE

He stood silently outside her door for a few minutes before retreating to the living room. The western decor in her home reminded him of that in his own parents' home. His mother loved leather furniture and western art. He ran his fingers over the top of a table-top bronzed sculpture of a mustang and rider. The depicted scene made him think of the early morning rides he used to take with Noah when they were in high school.

There was nothing like being out on the prairie at sunrise - seeing the way the sun melted away the darkness, bursting onto the horizon in a kaleidoscope of oranges, reds, and yellows. He didn't get to ride much during the school year, but once a month, necessity always made sure he got to see a sunrise. The moment when the colors exploded onto the sky was the same moment the magick released him from his animal form.

He eyed the front door. She'd told him to leave, but he couldn't do it. After all this time, he had a chance with her. For a few moments she'd let him comfort her, but then shut him out again. The bedroom door in his face had been a painful reminder that he had a long way to go to earn her trust.

His pocket buzzed. Pulling out his phone, he glanced at the screen and held it up to his face. "What's up, Noah?"

"Hey bro, her phone rang. She left it in our room with her clothes. So I answered it."

His brother's voice was unusually lifeless, and he was stalling. Noah never stalled; he'd been born telling it how it was since he was baby. Kind, but always honest and upfront.

"Noah."

"It was Houston PD. They were letting her know the remains of her parents were being released, and they wanted to know where to send them. Did she tell you her parents were dead?"

Goddess! Oh, fuck. Luke sank onto the cushion of the closest couch and hung his head. "No."

"No wonder she's so messed up, Luke. Man, I can't imagine getting that call and then finding out she was dating a jack-of-all-jills in the same night."

"Neither can I." He glanced toward the dark hallway, his heart breaking for the pain she was feeling. Her physical pain was fading as his essence worked quickly to heal her wounds from the accident, but these emotional wounds wouldn't fade nearly as fast. If ever. He couldn't fathom losing his mom or dad. Short of beheading, there wasn't much from which they couldn't heal. Werewolves lived a long, healthy life until their essence faded at their hundredth birthday.

"I gave them mom's number and called her. I tried not to give away anything to her, but she's suspicious. You know mom. Sorry, I didn't know what else to do."

Yes, he knew his mom. Nothing got past Tonya VonBrandt. "It's not like I could hide it anyway, Noah. It's fine."

"How is she?"

"Crying alone in her room. She tried to get me to leave, but I'm concerned, especially now that I know about her parents."

"You don't think she'll do anything, do you?"

"I don't think so, but I'm not taking any chances. I can't get a read on her emotions because... well..." The bond wouldn't be complete until he and Kara slept together, but until then he at least could feel anything she might try physically. The idea of her trying to hurt or even possibly kill herself made him sick. At least now he understood the dark cloud of depression and volatile emotional status that would make her run blindly in front of a vehicle. A cheating boyfriend was bad, but that's not what was truly upsetting her world. Vincent was just an extra piece of dog shit on top of the cow patty life had served up.

"Yeah, man. I get the idea. No leaving Kara alone. Comprende, bro. I'll stop by Pops' in a few hours and bring you some food and her phone and keys."

"Can you get into her room at KAS and get her purse? She said that was the only thing she might need from there."

"Will do. Later."

Luke shoved his phone back in his jeans pocket, got up, and walked to her bedroom door. He tried the handle and breathed a sigh of relief when it turned and the door pushed open.

The walls were a soft butter yellow, and there were sheets of country-western musical scores in frames decorating her walls. She had collected arrangements from George Strait and Dolly Parton to Blake Shelton and Miranda Lambert. Pictures of her in choir throughout high school filled in the gaps. She had a beautiful voice, but got terrible stage fright. Karaoke at Everyday Joe's wasn't the same without a number from Kara. The whole town loved her, but the only time they could get her to perform was after she'd downed a few drinks and been literally pushed onto the stage.

She was the first person to laugh or offer a smile to a stranger. She didn't deserve to go through this; to have her heart broken and then crushed at the same time.

Tiny sobs came from beneath a mountain of white

blankets and pillows.

"Kara," he said her name softly, moving to kneel beside the bed.

"Go away." Her voice was hoarse from the crying.

"No."

The bed moved and a pillow flew at his face. He batted it away and met her angry gaze.

"I don't want you here."

"Well, too bad. You've got me." Luke knelt to the floor and rested his elbows on the mattress. "In fact, you've got my whole family. Noah took a call on your phone from the Houston PD a few minutes ago."

"Shit!" The covers flew off the bed and she sat straight up in the center. "I left it at your frat house."

"It's okay. Noah is bringing it by. He's on his way." Luke paused, unsure of how to proceed. "He gave them our mother's number to call and help make arrangements to get them home."

She turned to face him slowly, her blue eyes burning through to his soul like fiery darts from hell. "How dare you involve your mother in my personal business? I barely even know you!"

"You know what!" He stood, surprised at her angry outburst. That was not the reaction he'd expected. Maybe a thank you, but definitely not a "fuck you".

He backed toward the bedroom door, shaking his

head. "You almost died in my arms last night. So pardon me for thinking you might need a little help," he continued, shouldering the responsibility for the choice to involve his family. To involve magick. In the end, all roads would lead back to him anyway. Might as well peel the bandaid off fast and get it over with.

"I feel like I almost died!" She screamed, crawling to the edge of the bed. She stood next to him, her eyes red from crying, her skin wrinkled from the sheets. "So why am I alive? And why the hell do I have the same crazy tattoos on my wrists that you have?"

"Noticed that, huh?" The forest green tattoos encircling her wrists were beautiful against her creamy white skin, but very obvious. It wasn't something she'd ever be able to hide.

She held up a hand, flipping him the bird at the same time. "They're hard to miss!" Stepping forward, she surprised him again with a forceful shove from both her palms flat on his chest. "What did you do to me?"

"I saved your life," he exclaimed, taking a step back to recover his balance. His mind was spinning. What did he say? Not say? How much should he explain?

"How? I can't find a single scratch on me, and yet my clothes were soaked down the back with my blood. And now I have weird Celtic-looking knot tattoos curling around my wrists. What in the bloody hell is going on?"

"Would you believe me if I said it was magick?"

She stopped in her tracks, mouth falling open. Then she giggled. It was a strange, somewhat crazy giggle, but a laugh all the same. It grew into a full-blown side-splitting roll.

Luke just stood and waited. Her emotions were a roller-coaster and he'd just sent her sailing over another drop off with the magick bombshell. That is, if she even believed him.

***

Kara laughed until her face hurt, but Luke just stood calmly —staring. It was unnerving. She gasped through a couple more chuckles and sat down on the edge of her mattress. Magick? She looked at him again. The crazy man was serious. She could see it in his eyes. Not even a hint of a smile tugged at the corners of his kissable lips.

Why am I thinking about kissing Luke VonBrandt? I just found out Vincent was cheating on me. I barely know this guy.

The thoughts didn't stray far. In fact she found herself imagining what Luke's body looked like underneath his clothes. It wasn't hard, since she'd had a quick peek at absolutely everything only a few hours ago. That had to be why she was obsessed with thinking about kissing him. Seeing a hot guy naked would make any girl think about it. *Right?*

Except that she should be thinking about her parents and everything she needed to do for them. She didn't even know where they wanted to be buried, or how. Where the money to pay for everything would come from. She'd never even talked to her mother about what to do if something happened.

Her whole world had collapsed on itself in one night.

Now she had one of the most eligible Greek Row bachelors, in her house, trying to help her, and she was being an absolute bitch with a capital 'B'. She'd known Luke for years. They'd gone to school together since they were in kindergarten. He didn't deserve this.

"I'm sorry," she murmured, tears beginning to fall down her cheeks again like water on a windshield. "I'm just so —" It didn't matter. She did need the help. And if he and his family were offering, she'd be a fool not to accept it.

He moved hesitantly, probably concerned she'd verbally or physically attack him again. A few more steps brought him to the bedside and he sat down next to her, cautiously wrapping his arm around her shoulder.

She leaned into his warm body and continued to sob. When the police had called the first time, she'd been alone. No one was around. And then, after seeing Vincent and Samantha together, the last few remaining brain cells in her head had ceased all sane thought processing.

"It's okay, Kara. I know it's a little outside of the norm. Plus, you've got to be exhausted."

Exhausted didn't even begin to describe how she felt. Besides feeling like she'd been run over by a truck - which she had - everything felt *off.*

"You seriously expect me to believe that a magick spell is healing me from getting hit by your truck?"

Luke sighed and squeezed her a little tighter. "Not just a spell. You are connected to me, to my essence... permanently. That's why we both have the bond marks now."

"Bond marks? The tattoos?"

He grunted an affirmation.

She grabbed his free hand and pulled it across his lap toward hers. Then put her wrist up next to his. The marks were identical. The same emerald green and even the knots were in the same places. His were thicker than hers, but the design was exactly the same.

"So when you said the spell the marks just appeared?"

"They slowly appeared, but yes," he replied.

"Who are you?"

He chuckled, his laughter sending relaxing vibes through her tense and anxious body. "Luke VonBrandt."

Kara pulled away from his arm and shoved him, nearly pushing him off the edge of the bed. "Shit! Sorry,

I didn't mean to push that hard."

He smiled, shaking his head. "It's fine."

"So really... who are you?"

"It would be better to wait a little while to explain things. Just know that I will always love, protect, and care for you, no matter what you choose after everything is said and done."

She scooted away from him, toward her padded floral print headboard. *Love? Protect? Care for?* Those words sounded like some sort of marriage proposal.

A glint of hurt flashed in his bright blue eyes. A second later it was gone. But she'd seen it. Her retreat had hurt his feelings as much as his statement had shocked and surprised her.

He stood from her bed and walked to the doorway. "I'll be right back. Noah's here with some food." He didn't look back. Just disappeared from sight.

Sure enough, a few moments later she heard Noah's voice in the entryway. How had he known Noah was here? She hadn't heard a car door or a knock on the door. His phone hadn't buzzed either.

"This is ridiculous." She wiped her face and took a deep breath. Her gaze fell on the marks on her wrists again, reminding her that even though she wanted this crazy story to be explained another way, there were too many things that just didn't add up to normal.

She crawled to the edge of her bed and stood again. Her mom and dad would be pissed that she was leaving guests alone in the house. A tiny smile tugged at her lips. She could hear her mother talking now, telling her to make sure they were offered a drink or something to eat, but a moment later, instead of a smile, more tears were trailing down her cheeks.

Squaring her shoulders and wiping the fresh tears from her face, she left her room and walked slowly down the hall. Noah and Luke fell silent as she approached. Her black hobo purse hung from Noah's right hand, meaning he had gone to her sorority room.

"How did you get in?" She pointed to the purse.

He lifted it out, and she took it from his hand. "I had your keys."

"No one said anything?"

"They did."

She raised her eyebrows in surprise. His shoving his way through a pack of KAS sisters would've been quite the spectacle. "Thank you." She hugged the purse to her chest and then set it gently on the entry table.

"Anytime." He lifted the bag in his left hand, displaying the Pops BBQ name on the side. "Brought lunch, too. Thought you might be hungry since you didn't get to eat the kolaches from earlier.

The sweet scent of honey BBQ sauce drifted to her nose, and her stomach growled. She hadn't eaten since lunch yesterday. It was barely eleven, but she wouldn't hold that against the BBQ.

"Thanks, Noah," Luke said before she could. He turned to her next. "Why don't you go sit down and let us fix you a plate?"

Both boys herded her toward the kitchen nook and refused to leave her side until she'd agreed to sit and let them fix her lunch.

She watched, amused, as they hunted through cabinets for dishes and utensils they needed. When she offered to get up and show them where things were they both snapped "no" in synchrony.

Within a few moments they were all three seated at the round kitchen table with a bounty of ribs, brisket, sliced turkey, link sausage, sweet creamed corn, rolls, cut green beans, and a bowl of tossed salad. It looked like enough to feed ten people, but as the guys dug in, she decided maybe it was just enough. Knowing what the VonBrandt's looked like underneath their wranglers and loose t-shirts, she wondered how they could look the way they did and eat the way they were eating. She couldn't blame them, though; their Pops made the best BBQ in town.

She kept her eyes on her food and tried not to think - about Luke, what'd happened, or anything for that matter. An empty brain was the goal. She needed a break from all the overwhelming emotions. Unfortunately, she had a feeling there was more to the story of her miraculous recovery than Luke or Noah was 'fessing up to.

Glancing up at them, her worries were confirmed when neither would make direct eye contact with her. It didn't matter right now. Her belly was full and she just wanted to forget everything, crawl back in her bed, and sleep. But there were too many things to take care of -- the house, bills, school ... her parent's funeral.

"I'm going to lie down." She got up and pushed in her chair. Both guys stood. "Thank you for the food. And for watching over me. I'll be fine though, if there's something else you need to do."

"Are you sure you ate enough?" Luke asked, glancing at her half-eaten plate.

"Yes," she said, nodding. "I'm so tired. Hopefully everything I need to do can wait one more day."

"What do you need?" Noah wiped his hands on a napkin and pushed in his chair. "I've got to go get books for my classes and run a couple of errands for mom. Luke is staying with you."

"He is, is he?" Kara raised an irritated eyebrow.

"Mom wanted you to come over to the house for dinner. I didn't want to leave you alone either." Luke VonBrandt met her glare head on.

She apparently didn't have a say in whether or not she was going to be looked after.

"Have you picked up your books for your classes yet?" Luke asked.

"No."

"Do you have your schedule? I'll pick them up and meet y'all at the house this evening."

"I don't have cash, and I can't let you go get all my books for me. I'm sure you have much better things to be doing than babysitting me. I'm fine. I promise. I just want to go lie down and sleep." She turned to leave, but then looked back at Luke. "I'm not sure I'm up for dinner with your parents tonight."

Luke nodded. "I'll let them know."

She nodded and left them at the table.

CHAPTER FOUR

Luke swallowed, trying to rein in his sinful thoughts as he watched Kara's hips sway softly from side to side. He'd gotten what he'd always wanted - a chance with Kara. But everything was fucked up. From the way he'd cast the bonding spell, to her parents' deaths, and the clusterfuck that was Vincent Harris.

He glanced at his brother and growled. Noah was grinning.

"You've got it bad for her."

"Shut it."

"You always have. But now you're bonded. What is that like?"

"Like having her right next to me all the time, but not being able to touch her. Plus, every time I look at her I want to throw her over my shoulder and find a big bed to crawl into."

Noah snorted and laid a hand on his shoulder. "I'm

gonna let you figure that one out. In the meantime, I think I saw her class schedule tucked in the front pocket of her purse. I'm going to go buy books. I'll drop hers by later."

"K."

"You know mom is coming over here if y'all don't go over there."

Luke sighed again. "It's a lot to take in all at once. It will probably be easier for her to just stay here instead of being bombarded by the VonBrandt pack."

"Be careful what you say. You haven't told her we turn into wolves, yet," Noah said softly before walking out of the kitchen. "She still thinks we just like to run buck naked in the woods."

Luke chuckled, then started clearing the table. There was still enough food left for several helpings. He found a few containers and packed the leftovers into the fridge. Then he washed and dried all the dishes they'd used for the meal. By the time he was finished, the kitchen sparkled and smelled lemon fresh.

Glancing around, he tried to find something else that might need to be cleaned or taken care of. His eyes trailed to the window at the back of the nook. The large backyard looked pretty tall. In fact, the front had looked even taller. The last thing he wanted was Kara to get a city notice for not having the grass mowed.

He pulled off his shirt and laid it over the back of one

of the kitchen chairs, then went through the back of the kitchen to the garage. At the front of the very organized two-car space was a bright red lawn mower. A weed-eater hung on the wall next to it.

An hour later he'd finished mowing both lawns and was finishing up the trimming along the street. The hair on the back of his neck stood up when Vincent's red pickup pulled to a stop across the street. The asshole brought Kara flowers? *Hell no!* Vincent started across the street with a bouquet of roses in his arms, but paused when he met Luke's gaze.

Luke let the lever go on the trimmer, and the gas-powered motor silenced. "Get lost, Vincent. She's resting, and she sure as hell doesn't want to see you."

Vincent continued approaching, ignoring him and heading for the sidewalk that led up to the front door.

Luke set the weed eater down and sprinted to cut him off.

"Get out of my way, rich boy. Kara is my girlfriend." He sneered. "She picked me over you back in high school, and you still can't get past it." Vincent moved forward, trying to use his shoulder to knock Luke out of the way.

"You've never deserved her. You cheated on her in high school, too. She deserves someone better."

"You?" Vincent laughed. "You think mowing her daddy's lawn is going to get you in their good graces?

Her parents love me. Move it." He tried to shoulder past again.

Luke growled and pushed Vincent hard enough to knock him backward onto his ass. "If you hadn't been fucking her roommate, you would've been there for her and know that her parents were killed in a car accident."

He loomed over the other guy and thrust out his chest angrily. "She's mine now. So get lost."

Vincent scrambled to his feet, leaving the roses spread across the freshly cut Bermuda grass, and charged, knocking them both to the ground. Vincent's fists crunched into his ribs twice before a female scream from behind them made them both freeze.

Shit! She'd felt the hits as if Vincent had hit her. When he'd goaded the jerk, he'd forgotten the spell went both ways. She wouldn't actually be bruised, but the pain would linger as if she were. *Damn it!*

He scrambled to his feet and hurried toward her. "Kara, I'm so sorry."

"Kara, baby, I didn't know." Vincent was right behind him.

Kara clutched her side, mirroring the pain he felt in his ribs.

"Get away from me." She shirked away from Luke's outstretched hand and turned her gaze on Vincent. She took a step toward the cheating asshole, and he thought his heart might stop from the shock.

"Baby, I'm so sorry about your parents. I would never --"

Her face hardened, and the soft sparkle in her blue eyes turned dark and angry. "I never want to see you again, Vincent Harris. Don't come near me. Don't speak to me. Ever. Again."

"But." Vincent's jaw dropped and he held his hands out. "We can work it out, baby."

"Fuck. Off. Vincent Harris."

"Bitch." Vincent shot back.

Luke snarled and clenched his hands into fists. He didn't throw a punch, though. It would only hurt and confuse Kara. The phantom pain from his being hit twice was enough. She was still bent a little to the side from the throbbing pain he was ignoring in his ribs.

A moment later Vincent turned and hurried back to his truck.

"As for you, Luke. I'm not yours either. I want you to put up the lawn stuff and leave my house."

What? "Kara. I don't feel comfortable --"

"Out. Now." Her body was taut and stiff. Anger radiated off her thicker than the humidity in the August Texas air.

He held up his hands in submission and backed away.

She turned around and slammed the front door behind her, the lock on the bolt sliding into place with a finality that made Luke sick to his stomach. He'd really screwed this up with her. He didn't know what to do to fix it, either. But the least he could do is what she asked. After putting away the weed eater and the lawnmower he hit the button on the side of the garage door and waited until it closed and locked in place.

He got into his truck and drove away slowly, watching the front door in his rearview mirror as long as possible. Everything inside him hoped she would open the front door and come out, arms open, forgiving him for whatever it was he'd done wrong.

***

What the hell is wrong with men? She couldn't believe Vincent had shown up again to try and win her back. With roses, too! Asshole. She never wanted to see him or her roommate again. She'd have to let the chapter president know she'd be moving out of the KAS house. Samantha could have her room and her boyfriend; she didn't need either anymore.

Then, Luke had gone all macho protector and shouted that she was his. His? What gave him the right to say that to anyone? Sure, he'd saved her life and they had these really weird matching tats, but they'd never been together before. They'd never even been on a date before.

The comment about Vincent being a cheater since the

beginning had been the last straw. How could she have been so blind? And if Vincent was that horrible and Luke was that interested, why the hell hadn't he said something before now? She'd wasted so much of her heart on a man that apparently didn't give a shit about her.

Right now, the last thing she wanted was another relationship. She just wanted to be alone. She wanted to cry and mourn her parents in peace. She wanted to finish school and make them proud, but she didn't even know how to make arrangements to get them back to Somewhere for a funeral.

She thought she'd loved Vincent, but saying goodbye to him after hearing everything Luke said outside was easier than she'd thought it would be. It made her sick to think he'd pulled the wool over her eyes for so long. How many other girls – friends - had he slept with since they'd started dating?

Wandering back to her room, she crawled back into her bed and burrowed under the fluffy comforter, blocking out the light from her window. She prayed sleep would come back quickly and carry her away from all the pain and tears threatening to pour down her face once more. The tears wouldn't stop. It didn't matter what came to mind, the tears always kept falling.

***

A knock at the door startled her from sleep. She threw back the covers and grimaced. It was dark outside. She must've slept for hours. Tucking her loose hair behind her ears, she rubbed her eyes and scooted to the edge of the bed.

Another firm knock echoed through the house.

"Coming," she hollered, scurrying down the hallway. She approached the door cautiously. It was nighttime, and she'd told the only people who knew she was here to get lost. Who in the world would be at her door?

Leaning closer, she peered through the peephole and gasped. It was Tonya VonBrandt, Luke's mother. She pulled open the door and stepped back, folding her arms across her chest. The woman looked like she might hug and kiss all over her, and that was the furthest thing from what she wanted. Actually, she didn't want anything from the VonBrandts at all.

"Noah asked me to give these to you." She held out a large McAdams University book bag filled with text books.

"I told him I could get my own books," Kara growled. "Your sons don't listen very well."

Tonya VonBrandt laughed and set the books down, leaning the bag against the wall. She shut the front door and then turned back to Kara. "When someone they care about is hurt, they don't listen to anyone."

"I barely know them. Or you, for that matter." Her voice was harsher than it should've been. Her mom would've been upset at her behavior. She looked back up at the tall woman in her entryway. Tonya VonBrandt had come all the way into town to bring her books, the least she could do was invite her to sit down.

"Come on in. Can I get you a glass of something?"

"No, baby girl, I'm fine. I need to talk to you about a few small details for your parents."

Tonya sat on the long couch, and Kara tucked herself into her dad's recliner across the room. She didn't want to be touched, and their mom looked like a touchy-feely sort of person. She'd certainly raised two boys who weren't afraid of hugging. Not that she'd minded the hugs from Noah or Luke, she just didn't want more of them. At least that's what she felt right now. The less she got attached, the less it would hurt when they got tired of being nice out of pity and left.

"I've made arrangements for a funeral at St. Joseph's on Sunday afternoon. Is that okay with you? I wasn't sure. I can contact the Catholic cathedral instead, if that would be better."

"My parents went to St. Joseph's. They would want it to be there."

"Good." Tonya pulled a small notebook and a pen from her purse. "It's set for 3pm on Sunday. I'll have a car pick you up so you don't have to drive. And it's just for you, unless you would like someone to ride with you."

"Why are you doing this for me?"

"My boys asked me to. Plus, no young woman should have to deal with this all by herself."

Kara watched the woman intently and noticed her gaze flit to her wrists and then back to her face.

"I also put in a call to my brother-in-law. He's a very good lawyer, and can help you with the estate and finances. So you can get everything transferred to your name without any trouble."

"I don't know how I can pay for all of this. I'm not even sure if my parents had life insurance. We never talked about what to do... if."

"That's why I'm here, sweetie. Don't worry about the money right now. That's not what's important. Do you know where your mom and dad might've kept important papers in the house?"

"They would be in her closet."

"Can you show me? It would help if we could look at some things before Jason comes by tomorrow."

Kara nodded and stood from the chair. She led Tonya down the hallway, past her bedroom to the door at the end of the hall. She opened it, stepped into her parents' bedroom, and took a deep breath. Tears welled in her eyes again as the scent of her mother's citrusy perfume hit her nostrils.

Tonya's hands touched her shoulders, and she stiffened at first, but then let her pull her into an embrace. "My mom and dad are gone," she sobbed into the other woman's soft blouse. "What am I going to do without them? I don't have anyone. My only aunt died last year."

"It's going to be okay, baby. Maybe not today or tomorrow. Maybe not even next week. But I promise it will get easier, and you are not alone, Kara McClure. You will have as much support from our family as you need."

Kara's body shook with each sob, and she took comfort from the soft touch of Luke's mother. Tanya VonBrandt ran her hand through Kara's hair a lot like Kara's mother used to whenever she was upset.

"Why? I'm not part of your family." She pulled away from Tonya and pointed to the closet door across the room. "I can't go in there, yet, but there's a file box in the back corner."

Tonya inclined her head toward Kara's wrists. "You're more part of our family than you realize yet. But that's not what's important right now. Right now, I just want you to know we are all here for you." She dropped her gaze and went to the closet, pulling open the door and disappearing into Kara's mother's walk-in.

She reappeared a few moments later with a large box. "I'm going to take these into the kitchen. Do you want to come sit with me and talk?"

Kara nodded and followed her back through the house.

They sat at the kitchen table, and Kara watched quietly as Luke's mom started pulling folders from the file box.

"Luke said the tattoos were because of a magick spell."

Tonya laid down the papers she was scanning over and sighed. "Did he say anything else?"

"Isn't that crazy enough?"

"Can you explain where you got the tattoos?"

"No," Kara answered, leaning back in her chair.

"Did he tell you why he cast the spell?"

Cast the spell? She's acting like this is normal. "He hit me with his truck."

"He did what!?" Tonya stood up, her eyes flashing angrily.

"It wasn't his fault," Kara added quickly. "I was running in the dark. I stumbled and fell into the street in front of him. He didn't have time to stop."

She slowly sank back to her seat. "What happened?"

"I'm not really sure. I remember hitting the grill and then nothing. But when I woke up later in his truck that night, I was covered in dried blood. Enough that I should've been dead, but couldn't find a single scratch."

"You won't. Luke's essence will heal any injury you receive as long as he lives."

"What does that even mean?" Kara leaned forward. "His essence?"

"My husband's family comes from a long line of ... something very special." She unbuttoned the cuffs of her long sleeve shirt, revealing a set of tattoos around her wrists that looked very familiar.

She looked at her wrists and then back at Tonya's. The tattoos were similar. Both Celtic with knots, but the designs were a little different. The biggest difference was that Tonya had double bracelets and Kara only had one knotted bracelet design around each wrist.

"I don't understand." Kara looked up into the soft brown eyes of Luke and Noah's mother.

"Luke can cast this spell only once in his life. It's something that's normally included in wedding vows. I understand why he used it to save your life, but you need to understand what he's sacrificed. You will both be magickally connected until one or both of you pass away."

"This isn't a joke, is it?"

"No, sweetheart. It's not a joke."

"There's more going on than just this tattoo essence weirdness."

The corners of Tonya's mouth turned up, but she quickly hid her amusement. "Why do you think there's more than an old binding spell?"

"Because this spell doesn't explain why I saw Luke and Noah this morning walking naked through the woods when I woke up in his truck."

"No, I suppose that is a little harder to explain. I also think it might be best for you to adjust to one VonBrandt family secret at a time." She pulled another folder from the file box and opened it up on the table, sifting through paper after paper. "I found your parents' life insurance."

It was just a way to change the subject. Kara's mom had been a pro at redirecting conversations, too. But it was fine. She'd go along with it for now. She still didn't want to have anything to do with Luke right now, but maybe... in time.

"Do you think it's enough to cover the funeral?"

Tonya nodded and met her gaze. "Yes, dear. Your parents made sure you had more than enough to bury them and take care of yourself for quite a long time as long as you manage the money well. And that's just the life insurance. I haven't found the bank statements yet. Jason will be able to explain everything much better than I can. I just wanted to determine whether you needed money right away or not."

"You were going to give me money? Why?"

"I told you, Kara. You are part of the family now."

CHAPTER FIVE

The next morning, Kara woke to find her car keys on the kitchen table and a note beside them.

Wanted to be sure you had your car. Forgot we still had your keys, too. Please call if you need anything. I know you don't want to see me, but just know that if you change your mind, I'll be around. --Sincerely, Luke

She poured herself a bowl of bran flakes and a glass of OJ. Then she sat down at the table and tried not to cry as she ate. *Damn it.* He was being so thoughtful. The whole family was. Noah had helped her. Luke had helped her. God, Luke had saved her life. Then, even his mother had stepped in, called a lawyer, and gone through her mom's papers herself.

Still, she just couldn't deal with him right now. Every time she looked at him, she just wanted to rip his clothes off and get another look at his chiseled body. There must be something psychologically wrong with her. How could a person be so overwhelmed with grief and yet so turned on at the same time? She was weepy and wanted to hide from the world, but her mind wouldn't let her stop thinking about Luke.

It couldn't happen. Not right now.

She needed time to grieve. Time to get her life in order. School started on Monday. And thanks to Noah's inability to listen, she had books and study guides for every single class she was taking. They sat in neat little piles on the coffee table. She'd gone through the bag Tonya had brought before she went to bed last night. He'd even bought her a pack of pens and a half-dozen composition notebooks.

It was above and beyond.

She finished her cereal, washed out the bowl in the sink, and padded through the silent house, back to her room. It was Saturday. She should be at the sorority house prepping for Greek week. *Nope. I'm calling it quits on the KAS house.* Her only other responsibility was working up at Everyday Joe's. She needed to call him and let him know she couldn't work this weekend. Not unless he wanted her crying into the customers' drinks every five minutes.

It was going to be hard enough to keep it together for classes on Monday.

She grabbed her phone off the small white nightstand and sank down onto the mattress, dialing Joe's cell. He probably wasn't even awake yet. The phone rang twice before it picked up.

"Hello?" An unfamiliar female voice answered the phone.

Kara pulled her phone back and check the caller id to make sure she hadn't misdialed. *Nope.* The screen read Joe's Cell.

"Is Joe there?"

The voice grunted and called out Joe's name, telling him someone named Kara was on the line. She heard the phone transfer to another hand and then his froggy voice come on the line.

"Kara, baby girl, do you know how early it is?"

"Sorry, Joe." She sniffed and tried not to break into tears. "I just... I can't work this weekend. My parents were k-killed in a car accident. I need to -"

"Shit! Kara!" His voice changed from mildly annoyed to concerned in record speed. "Baby girl, I'm so sorry. Don't worry your pretty head about the bar. Hear me? You take the weekend off. Hell, the whole week. Whatever you need."

"K, thanks, Joe. S-sorry about waking you."

"It's nothing. Get some rest and call me if you need anything. I mean it. I'll bring you some food, alcohol, whatever."

She smiled. He was the biggest player in town, but he

really did have a heart of gold. Which was part of the reason he could get into just about any panties in town. At least he kept it professional at the bar. He had a rule about not sleeping with anyone he employed.

"I'm good, Joe. I've got enough food in the house for now. Thanks."

"Alright, but the offer still stands. Just call. When is the funeral?"

"Tomorrow at St. Joseph's. 3pm."

"I'll be there, baby girl. Don't do anything today. Just rest."

"I will. Bye, Joe."

"Bye."

She dropped the phone from her ear and tapped the end button on the screen, then let the phone drop on the mattress next to her. She scooted to the center of her bed and curled up, pulling the sheet and comforter up over her head. Resting today sounded like the best idea to her, too. It was still early. She could do stuff later... if there was something that needed to be done.

Tonya had said she'd do everything for the funeral, and they'd talked about details last night before she left.

Out of all the people she could've stumbled in front of, she'd fallen in front of Luke VonBrandt. Now, according to his mother, they were linked for life whether she liked it or not. Tonya had explained the phantom pain she'd felt when Luke and Vincent had fought yesterday. Apparently, they could feel each other's physical injuries. So those punches Vincent had thrown into Luke's ribs felt like they re-broke hers. They hadn't, and surprisingly they were barely even tender now.

It shouldn't surprise her. Her body had hit a moving pickup truck. She'd likely had broken bones, internal injuries, and from the way the bloodstains had trailed down her clothes, she must've had a head injury.

Holy crap! Did that mean he could feel all of that after he said the spell?

***

Luke paced back and forth in his room at the AKO house. The bond assured him that Kara was safe, but he was dying to go over to her house and check up on her. He couldn't *not* think about her. Even his wolf was mopey and depressed. They both craved the connection. If she didn't forgive him for acting like a Neanderthal and fighting Vincent in her front yard, life would cease to hold any meaning whatsoever. That might be a tad dramatic, but this spell was doing a number on him.

He'd known casting the spell would start something he had no control over, but he hadn't thought it would be this bad. No wonder the spell was traditionally cast at wedding ceremonies.

He groaned and ran his hands through his shaggy black hair.

"Chill, bro. You're gonna wear a hole in the carpet." Noah stood from the recliner in front of the TV and approached him. "Wanna go for a run?"

"Yeah, maybe it will distract my brain."

"We can hope." Noah chuckled. "But I'm not sure anything could distract me if I were bonded to Kara McClure either."

"I thought you were trying to help," Luke growled.

Noah slipped into his tennis shoes and grinned. Luke shook his head and huffed out a breath of frustration.

"Come on, bro. We can run by her house if you want, even though I don't recommend it. Mom said she didn't give any indication that she wanted you around."

"Patience is your thing, Noah. Not mine." Luke smiled at his brother. "Maybe just a quick run by her house. We won't stop."

Noah laughed again and shrugged.

They took the stairs down two at a time. The guys in the living room barely looked up from the sports game on the big screen. Luke paused at the doorway.

"Grant." He waited for the big guy at the end of the couch to look at him. "Noah and I will be back in a couple of hours. Have the first-years spin the chore wheel and be done by the time we get back."

"No prob. Maid service will commence in three. Two. One."

Luke grinned at the groan from several of the guys sprawled on the floor. He nodded to Grant and then met his brother out on the porch.

Noah looked up. "Toilet torture?"

"Yep." He jogged down the front path and leapt into a steady pace.

His brother hollered from the porch and pounded the pavement behind him, quickly catching up and falling into sync with his stride. Luke loved running. The rush of the endorphins, whether wolf or man, was exhilarating.

He took a deep breath of the sweet summer air. Somewhere, Texas was clean and just small enough that no one really paid attention to the fact that his family disappeared from time to time. If he was careful, he could even get away with shifting during the day.

They ran in silence, their strides beating the pavement in a hypnotic rhythm. The burn in his legs distracted him from the ache in his soul. It only took ten minutes to reach her house.

He stopped in front of it, even though he'd told Noah he wouldn't.

Noah stopped too, but didn't speak.

"I can feel her there...but nothing else."

"She'll come around, Luke. Just give her some time.

Imagine how messed up we would be if we found out mom and dad were just gone." He snapped his fingers and frowned. "She's got to find her way through all this before she can reach out to you."

Luke shook his head. "Who went and made you Yoda?"

"The girl, find you, she will." Noah croaked out, doing his best to keep a straight face.

A laugh exploded from Luke's chest. "Come on, you big dork. Let's get out of here before she sees me stalking her."

Noah chuckled and fell into step next to him.

***

Laughter outside had drawn Kara to the window next to the front door. She peered through a crack in the drapes, watching Luke and Noah VonBrandt disappear down the sidewalk.

She'd known it was him before she looked. How, she wasn't sure. But something inside her knew. Something new. She could feel his heartbeat race as he ran, feel the jolt to his body with each step. The sensations hadn't made sense until she saw them outside. But now all the sensations made sense - running.

It shouldn't be possible. But it was happening.

She turned from the window. Misjudging her step, she stubbed her toe on the entry table leg. "Shitake mushrooms!" she hissed, and hopped on one leg. But one mishap turned into another. Losing her balance, she fell backward, slamming her back into the wall and slipped to the floor with a thud. Another curse slipped out and then a laugh. The laughter quickly turned to tears. She shouldn't find her clumsiness funny. How could anything be funny right now, especially getting hurt?

A harsh knock on the door made her shriek. *What the hell?*

Then she felt him.

"Kara?" His voice called out, filled with tension. "Kara, are you okay?"

He'd felt her get hurt, just like she was able to feel him running. It didn't matter that she didn't want to see him. Check that; her body might, but her brain needed time.

"I'm fine. Go away," she hollered through the closed door.

"Kara?"

Persistent little streaker, isn't he?

She smiled at her own sarcasm. Even though she didn't want to see him, it felt nice to have the distraction. At least for a few minutes.

"I'm going back to bed. Leave. Please."

The distraction was finished. She wanted her soft bed and comforter again. Ignoring his knocking, she hurried back to her room.

Sleeping was the least painful state. Her body didn't hurt once she drifted into unconsciousness, and only there could she forget that her parents were gone. She saw her mom and dad in her dreams. They were laughing and carrying on at the dinner table. Playing scrabble with her late into the night on the weekends. Cooking out with the neighbors for the Fourth of July weekend block party. It was like a movie reel of her favorite moments in her life when she slept. It was the only happy place she had right now.

Tomorrow she would have to face them at the funeral. The finality of the burial terrified her. She knew they were gone already, but she hadn't seen their bodies. Hadn't had to look at a casket. Hadn't had to speak with the pastor about the service. Tonya VonBrandt had taken care of everything - like a mom.

The mom she didn't have anymore.

She closed her bedroom door and then crawled back into her bed. The covers welcomed her back, cocooning her in a feather-soft mountain.

The knocking had stopped. At least Luke had given up for now.

She grabbed a pill from her nightstand drawer, sleeping aids she'd dug out of her mom's bathroom cabinet. Placing it on her tongue, she grabbed the small glass of water from the top of the nightstand and took a quick gulp. The pill didn't want to go down. It stuck in her throat, and she coughed before she took another sip. Finally it cleared, and she finished the rest of the water anyway.

It was time to disappear. Her mom always said not even the dead rising could disturb her after one of her pills. Kara hoped it was true. Tired didn't even begin to describe how she felt. Empty might be a more accurate description. There was nothing left to give.

She didn't want to feel anything right now. Even if it was only for the rest of the day.

CHAPTER SIX

Kara stared at herself in the bathroom mirror. Her long, blonde hair was brushed back and braided down the center of her back. She'd put on a little makeup, but nothing heavy. Most of it would run immediately from the onslaught of tears already waiting to fall. Even now her vision was blurred from the water pooling in her eyes.

She ran her hands down the simple black dress she'd dug out of the back of her closet. It fell just below her knees and clung to her curvy figure a little more than her mom would appreciate, but it was the only black dress she had. Her mom had several, but nothing she could fit. Plus, it seemed morbid to borrow something of her mom's.

A knock at the door snapped her out of her thoughts, and she took a deep breath. She'd slept straight for a day and a half. It was time to face the world again. She'd missed a couple of calls from Joe, but that was all. His messages had been sweet. Just checking up on her, seeing if he needed to bring her a bottle of anything.

She shook her head. Sleeping to avoid her feelings wasn't much different than opting to drink them away. She couldn't give him a hard time for having his way to deal.

With soft steps she walked to the front door and opened it wide. A tall man stood quietly behind dark sunglasses, a black dress suit, white dress shirt, black tie, and a pair of shiny black dress shoes. He gestured to the town car waiting at the curb.

She grabbed her small purse from the entry table and closed and locked the door behind her before following him down the walk. It occurred to her to ask his name or thank him for picking her up, but then decided against it. Small talk was unimportant. She'd rather sit quietly in the back of his car than try to converse. Likely he already knew exactly who she was and what had happened to her parents. Tonya had hired him, after all. She would've told him anything he needed to know. Pulling the purse to her side, she slipped into the backseat after he opened the door for her. When he closed it a single tear fell down her cheek.

It was happening. She was finally going to have to say goodbye to her parents. For real. The time for pretending was over. Life would have to go on. School started tomorrow. She couldn't afford to miss classes or fail because she was an emotional wreck. Then there was all the money and finance stuff that her parents left her. How was she supposed to know what to do and when?

The car started to move.

She glanced up into the rearview mirror. With the big sunglasses he was wearing, it was difficult to tell if he returned her gaze. As much as she didn't want to talk, she needed a connection with someone. He was a stranger, someone she wouldn't likely see ever again. But she changed her mind and wiped her face, turning to look out the window just in case he'd seen her crying.

"A funeral is a time to grieve for those we've loved and lost. We pay our respects publicly so the world knows how much they meant to us. Do not be embarrassed to express your emotions."

Her breath caught in her throat at his words. He had been watching her. Listening. "I'm afraid if I let myself start, it will never stop."

"It will. Just be sure you let someone watch over you. It's not good to be alone."

A hoarse chuckle shook her body. "Too late for that. I think I've already chased away anyone who might have cared to spend time with me."

"I think you are writing him off too easily." The deep voice of the driver rumbled on, soothing her frayed nerves. *Maybe he will offer to come home and sit with me after the funeral so I can cry until I pass out.*

Wait. Him who? Luke? How much did this driver

know? Wasn't he just a car driver?

"What's your name?"

He lowered his glasses for a second and caught her gaze in the rearview mirror again. His bright brown eyes were soft and compassionate. They reminded her of her father's. "Aaron VonBrandt, at your service, sweetheart."

"You're ..." She sucked in a quick breath and looked down at her hands clasped tightly in her lap. The strange green tattoos glared up at her, reminding her that there was a lot more going on in this family than anyone had shared so far. Worse than the obvious connection to his son, permanently stamped on her skin, Luke's father was the driver. One of the richest men in Texas was driving her around like her personal chauffeur.

"I wouldn't have trusted you with anyone else." The car lurched as they pulled into the lot behind St. Joseph's and parked. "I know my son has a great challenge ahead of him to gain your trust, but in the meantime, I want you to know that Tonya and I consider you part of our family. If you ever need anything, even if you want to stay the night at the ranch, instead of being alone. We have guest rooms ready and available to you at a moment's notice."

More tears fell, dropping from her cheeks to her hands. She wiped her cheek with the back of one of her hands and choked back a sob. She'd done nothing to deserve the kindness they were showing. In reality, she knew she should be dead, and poor Luke would've probably been put on trial for accidental manslaughter. The truth was, she'd come crashing into the VonBrandt's life, and they were having to clean up after her. But instead of making her feel like a burden or a nuisance, they were treating her like one of their children.

He got out of the car, opened her door, and knelt down, taking both her hands into his large palms. He took his sunglasses off and tucked them inside his suit jacket. Big brown eyes met her gaze. She blinked away her tears and tried not to completely come apart.

"Come, sweetheart. I'm so sorry about your parents." He tugged gently, guiding her from the back seat of the car. He slipped her arm around his elbow and let her lean on him as they walked across the lot toward the front door of the church.

He was strong, much taller than her father. But he had that same comforting touch. The one that made her feel safe. Protected. Loved.

She pushed back her tears and held her head high as they walked into the church. There were people everywhere. Some she recognized. Some she didn't.

Her senses tingled, and she scanned the room, looking for him. Heat swirled in her body, confusing her even more. Why did he affect her so much? She saw Tonya and Noah first. Luke was standing behind them, closer to the wall, putting as much distance between himself and her as humanly possible. He looked miserable. His blue eyes were distant, and his shoulders were hunched. Their eyes caught for a second before he looked away. Sadness was the dominant emotion painted on his gorgeous face.

She needed to talk to him. Maybe tomorrow at school.

Aaron VonBrandt led her through the crowd toward the main sanctuary door. She glanced over her shoulder once more, but Luke had disappeared from the wall. Her heart dropped a little, and she wondered where he'd gone.

They entered the sanctuary, and her thoughts left Luke, focusing on the pair of coffins sitting in front of the altar. Beautiful portraits of her parents were displayed on a small table between the two white coffins. There were pictures of them on their vacation to Florida last year, as well.

She pulled her arm free from Aaron and hurried down the main aisle. Tears blurred her vision and she struggled with one of the coffin covers, trying to lift it. One last look. She'd been cheated the chance to say goodbye.

Aaron laid his hand over hers and shook his head. "You want to remember them that way, Kara." He inclined his head toward the photo.

A sob tore from her throat. "I didn't get to say goodbye. I just need to say goodbye."

He shook his head and pulled her hand back from the

coffin.

"It's not fair!" Her voice rose in decibel. Control was fleeing her grasp. She hugged herself, taking a step backward. She couldn't focus through the tears pouring from her eyes.

"Kara." Luke's voice flowed over her like warm honey, coating her in a calm comfort she hadn't felt since he'd left her Friday.

She turned about and found herself only inches from his chest. Looking up, their eyes met, and she shivered as an electrical charge seemed to pass between them.

He stood frozen for a few moments before he lifted his hands up to her arms, tentatively, as if waiting for her to shirk away from his touch.

She didn't, though.

As much as she had promised herself she would avoid him, her body was betraying her. She leaned against his chest and took a deep breath through the shaking of her sobs. He smelled clean with a little spice from a cologne she couldn't identify, but it suited him perfectly.

His arms encircled her, drawing her tighter to his chest. Her ear was pressed against his chest and she listened to the *thump thump* of his heart and breathed. Just breathed. In and out. Time waited for her to catch her breath.

When she finally looked up at him again, he kissed

her forehead tenderly. His lips were warm and soft on her skin. And she felt the connection between them surge with life. She needed him to get through this.

At least for today.

Maybe it would be easier tomorrow.

Probably not.

***

Hope soared in his heart when she let him touch her, let him place a small kiss on her head. It wasn't a lot, but it was more than he'd expected. When his dad had walked into the church and she'd looked at him the first time in the lobby, there had been so much pain in her eyes. He could see it clawing up from her soul, choking the life from her. It killed him to see her that way and not be able to give her comfort.

He wanted nothing more in his life than to see her happy. If it meant staying away, he would do that too, but when her cries had carried through the sanctuary and he'd seen her backing away from his dad, something inside him had snapped.

He'd run to her side, swiftly and silently. Her name had left his lips unbidden. More a plea than a greeting. Then she had moved against him. She hadn't told him to leave. She hadn't backed away from his touch.

Maybe. Just maybe she would give him another chance.

He would do anything for that. Including stand here at the foot of the altar, holding her close, until she gave an indication she was ready to move.

The pastor had walked past and he'd shaken his head, sending him away. Stalling, doing what he could to help her feel more comfortable. She wasn't ready yet. Her arms were tucked tightly between her body and his. If they'd been alone and circumstances different, he would've scooped her up and carried her away. Away from her pain... if it were only possible. But the loss of her parents would not be something she recovered from quickly, and it was not something he could carry her away from, either.

So, for right now, he would appreciate that she trusted him enough to let him comfort her in the small way he could right now. In this moment, a hug was what she needed most of all.

He would be her constant, if only she would let him. He'd always wanted her. Always loved her from afar. Watching her date that jerk had made him throw himself into his studies just to keep his mind off the fact that she wasn't his and might never be.

His mother and father had listened silently last night as he'd told them what had happened that fateful full moon. They'd known he'd liked Kara for a long time, and both understood why he hadn't been able to let her die, but both had also voiced concern that she might never return his feelings. They'd asked him if he was prepared to live his life without her, if that's what she chose.

He'd told them yes, but he knew both he and his wolf would never rest easy until she slept in his arms every night. Until she was his. Heart and soul.

People started to file into the sanctuary. The clock on the back wall showed the time was a few minutes after three. He'd stalled the service as long as he could.

The pastor gestured toward a pew and he nodded.

"Kara, we need to sit." He spoke slowly and nudged her toward the first row of pews, just to his right.

She tensed in his arms for a second and then moved to sit. He sank down on the pew next to her without speaking another word. She didn't make eye contact with him or anyone else. Her gaze remained frozen, locked on the photo of her parents smiling in the Florida sun. Palm trees waved in the background behind them, and the white sandy beaches sparkled and flashed.

The pastor started the service, and Kara sat still and quiet as he spoke about her parents. About their love for life and their love for their daughter. The congregation stood to sing a hymn. Then a couple more people went to the podium to speak, telling a fond memory of Tom and Anna McClure. How much they were loved and how much they would be missed.

Still Kara didn't speak. All he could hear was the *thump thump* of her heart and the very soft intake and exhalation of her breaths. There were no sobs. Only a steady stream of tears dropped from her cheeks to her lap.

The service wrapped up with another hymn about crossing the Jordan and then the pastor dismissed the congregation.

Luke stood and offered his hand to Kara. She took it blindly and walked with him down the aisle and out of the church. He took her to the black town car in which his dad had driven her there.

"Do you want to ride by yourself?"

She didn't respond, so he leaned down and turned her to face him.

"Kara?"

Her beautiful eyes were empty, void of any emotion, and she wouldn't make eye contact. Instead she seemed to stare straight through him. Then a second later she connected.

"Please don't leave." Her voice was barely a whisper. "It's easier with you here."

He nodded and opened the passenger door. After helping her get in, he closed the door and turned to his father and mother. Noah stood a few feet away as well.

"Dad, will you drive?"

His dad pulled his sunglasses from his coat pocket and nodded. "Don't get pushy, Luke. She's got a longer way to go than you realize."

Luke nodded. He knew.

The ride to the gravesite was slow and torturous. Taking his cues from Kara, he remained silent, and so did his father. Once they arrived, Luke helped her out of the car again and walked her to the two sites that had been prepared for her parents. He and his family were the only ones that stood with her other than Joe Walker. The bartender was a player but a good guy at heart, and really cared about the people in the town. He knew everybody... and probably everything about them, too.

A bagpipe player walked up to the side of the grave and began to play. Luke glanced over to his mom. Tonya VonBrandt smiled. Kara's parents had been so proud of their Scottish ancestry. This tribute was something they would've really appreciated.

Kara's tears had started again. The sobs came in waves now, each cry crashing against his heart like the lash of a whip. He sensed her knees buckling and slipped an arm around her waist, holding her firmly against his side without any strain. She was so small.

The drone of the pipes split the afternoon air, touching his soul. There was nothing on earth quite like the sound of well-played bagpipes. The song was slow, stately, and yet seemed to soar on the air like a spiraling bird, lifting his spirits and hopefully Kara's.

The coffins were lowered, and the graves filled.

The piper continued seamlessly from one song to the next. Near the end of the fourth song, the graves had been filled and Kara straightened.

She had to be exhausted from the crying, but she didn't say a word. Just let him lead her back to the car.

He helped her in and then circled around to the other side to sit next to her. She whispered a thank you under her breath, but didn't look at him.

Luke took her left hand, damp from tears, into his hand and squeezed.

CHAPTER SEVEN

Numb. That's what she was now.

The pressure from Luke's hand on hers was heavy, but she couldn't feel it. Couldn't tell if his hand was warm or cold. Soft or hard. It was just there.

She couldn't look at him either. Her body sagged against the seat, and she watched the familiar landscape pass by - grass, trees, mostly oak and pecan. She couldn't tell how much time passed between leaving the cemetery and Luke's father pulling to a stop in front of her parents' house.

The bagpipe player at the graveside had been a wonderful tribute to her parents. Her mom and dad both would've loved it. But it'd also broken her steeled composure and she'd turned into a weeping mess. After they left, it was like she was just empty again.

She was awake, but not really. Just going through the motions.

When she looked up again she was standing in her bedroom staring at herself in the mirror above her vanity. Her face was splotchy, tear streaked, and what little make up she'd worn was completely washed away.

"Kara?" Luke stood in the doorway. "Kara?" he repeated.

How many times had he said her name? She looked up at him, but didn't know what to say. Something in his face changed from hesitant to protective in the space of a few seconds. His face remained solemn, but his eyes softened and caressed her in the way only a man's could.

He walked to her dresser and opened and closed the drawers until he found a pair of yoga pants and an oversized college t-shirt. "You need to change and lie down for a while."

She looked at the clothes in his outstretched hand, but still couldn't move. More tears flowed down her cheeks, and she turned her focus to the floor. It didn't matter if she changed. She could sleep in this dress. Moving to crawl into the bed, she felt his hands encircle her waist and pull her back.

"I'll help you, Kara," he murmured.

She straightened in front of him, quite aware that her backside was rubbing against his groin. They stood frozen for a moment. Then she felt his hands drift up her back to the top of the zipper. She held her breath. Was he going to undress her? Really?

He pulled at the zipper and ran it down the length of her back all the way to the curve of her ass. At least he had to step back to complete the task. She wasn't sure how much more of feeling his growing erection against her ass she could handle.

She shouldn't be aroused right now or thinking about his cock. But she was, and she couldn't stop. Each brush of his fingertips along her skin awakened her even more, awakened a need inside her that wanted to be sated. That wanted to disappear into the bliss and sanctuary that sex could provide - at least temporarily.

Grabbing the top of her dress, she yanked it down and shimmied until it pooled on the floor. She kicked off her high heels, losing three inches of height in the process. It didn't matter. She would get what she wanted tall or short. He wanted her too. That she was sure of.

Turning to face him, she pressed herself against his chest and reached for his face, pulling it down to hers. She covered his mouth with hers and pushed her tongue between his lips.

For a second he was unmoving, but his shock didn't last long. His arms encircled her body, pulling her tightly to him. He slid his hand up her back and dug into the hair at the base of her skull. Taking control of the kiss, he swept his tongue into her mouth and moaned.

Fire licked through her body, and she shivered in anticipation. This is what she needed. To forget the pain.

To forget her life. She wanted to disappear into him. Luke made everything feel better. His touch alone had calmed her in the church. Now his touch heated her body, and she wanted more.

Her hands flew to his belt. In a few short moments his belt was off and his pants were open. She reached inside to rub his cock. God, he felt nice. Hard and long, and yet as soft and smooth as velvet. Moisture pooled in her sex, and her body throbbed.

"Wait," he growled against her mouth and pulled away. "I can't do this. You'll hate me after. Kara, I can't."

He stepped backward a few steps, pulling up his pants and searching the floor for where she'd thrown his belt. A few seconds later he'd found that, too, and was completely dressed again.

She stood, shaking, in the center of her room. Her bra and panties still in place and Luke barely able to look at her. Was she that horrible? That unattractive? Vincent had cheated on her for years after all. Maybe there was something wrong with her. Maybe she was bad in bed? Or a bad kisser?

Looking up at him again, she seethed this time. Her hands clenched at her sides. No. He'd wanted her. She could feel it plain as day in the palm of her hand not ten seconds ago. What the fuck was wrong with him?

"Get. Out."

"Kara."

"Get. Out."

He nodded and left her room in a hurry, shutting the door behind him on his way out.

She sank down onto the edge of her mattress and dug her fingers into the comforter. The desire to tear something apart raged through every cell of her body. She threw her body down, burying her face in a pillow, and screamed. Again and again and again.

When the urge to scream had passed she picked up the clothes he'd laid on the bed and walked with them into the bathroom. Maybe a shower would help clear her mind and cool her still thrumming body.

***

Luke stood in the hallway just outside her door silently cursing himself. He'd heard her muffled screams of frustration. And then he'd heard the water turn on in the bathroom.

At least she was moving around. That was something.

It'd killed him to tell her no.

When she turned and kissed him, all clear thought vanished in an instant. He'd wanted to kiss her for so long. Wanted to feel her body against him. Then she was right where he wanted her. She'd taken him out of his pants and held his cock, squeezing just enough that he'd had to steel himself against grabbing her and throwing her down on the bed.

She was heaven. Everything he could've imagined. But it wasn't right. She was grieving. If they'd slept together then, it would've been a mistake. She would've hated him for taking advantage of her. Her emotions were so volatile right now. He knew she was looking for an escape.

He wanted to be that for her, but he wanted her long-term, not just to fuck and cast off. She was so much more to him than that. She needed to know that. He wanted to give her time to get to know him, to care about him. To want more than to use him as a temporary haven from her feelings.

His back rubbed the wall as he sank to the floor in the hallway, praying he hadn't ruined his only chance with her. His mom always told him to go with his gut, and his gut had screamed that meaningless sex was a mistake. His wolf was pissed at the missed opportunity to seal the bond completely, but *he* knew they needed more. It wouldn't have been fair to throw her another curveball until she was ready for it. The rush of emotions from the sealed bond might've sent her careening over a line from which he couldn't pull her back.

He closed his eyes and took a deep cleansing breath. "One step at a time."

The water finally shut off in the bathroom, and he listened to her move around for a few minutes before the bed squeaked. *Good.* She was at least trying to get some rest.

He climbed up from the floor and moved to lie on the couch in the living room. Turning on the TV crossed his mind, but mostly he wanted a nap as well. Several minutes later he felt himself drifting off.

***

Kara opened her eyes and stretched. She peeked at the clock on her nightstand and growled. *7:22pm.* She'd slept the whole afternoon away. It had been a restful sleep, though. The frustrations and emotional overload from earlier seemed better.

A little guilt gnawed at her heart over what she'd done to Luke.

She climbed out of bed and walked from her bedroom out into the living room. Slow steady breathing came from the couch, and she peered over the back. Luke hadn't left her alone, even after she'd been so hateful and confused. She'd practically tried to strip him naked earlier and ravish him. A small smile pulled at the corners of her mouth at the thought. He'd acted like sleeping together was a terrible idea, but something told her he was holding back... for something.

His face was beautiful. A square jaw, strong mouth, and angular face accented his masculinity. His shirt had come untucked, and a trail of dark hair led her eyes down his chiseled stomach toward his groin. The hair disappeared beneath the waist of his dress pants, but she already knew what lay hidden beneath a couple layers of fabric. He was built like one of those gladiators in that popular TV show playing on cable. She licked her lips and had to stop herself from reaching out to touch him.

Her stomach grumbled, and she turned away from the sexy man sleeping on her couch. Thoughts of caressing his features fled as her attention turned to her cramping stomach. She'd barely eaten all weekend and for once she was truly hungry.

A quick perusal of the fridge produced some leftover BBQ from Pops. She warmed the sliced turkey in the microwave and toasted a couple pieces of bread. After spreading a little BBQ sauce on the bread she put together her sandwich, grabbed a ginger ale from the fridge, and took a seat at the kitchen table.

The tangy scent of the sauce made her mouth water. She took a bite and sighed. It tasted good. Really good.

Movement in the living room caught her attention. Luke walked toward the kitchen and leaned against the doorway. He raised his arms up above him, baring most of his lower torso and stretched, pulling first one arm behind his head and then the other.

"Any left?" He eyed her sandwich hungrily.

"It's in the fridge. Help yourself." She took another bite. "The bread is in the basket next to the toaster," she added after swallowing.

"Thanks."

A few minutes later he joined her at the table with his own sandwich and a beer from the fridge. He'd also grabbed a bag of potato chips from the bread basket.

The salty scent of the chips made her mouth water, and she reached for the open bag. He pushed it closer to her and she whispered a thank you. She took a small handful and added them to her nearly empty plate. Her sandwich was all but finished.

"Can I get you anything else?" he asked. "I think I saw some fruit in the fridge too."

She shook her head. "This is good. Thanks."

He nodded and leaned back in the chair.

She could tell he wanted to say something, but again... something held him back. It was the same hesitant look he'd shown in the bedroom a few hours ago.

"Why didn't you want to sleep with me?"

A cough rattled in his throat and she swore his cheeks reddened a little.

"It's not that I didn't, Kara. I just -" He looked away, staring out one of the nook windows into the back yard. "You've been through hell the last few days, and I just don't think it's fair to put even more on your shoulders."

She ate the last chip on her plate and then leaned back in her chair, folding her arms over her chest. He was right. But she still wanted to sleep with him. In fact, it was the only thing she thought about when her mind wandered. Embarrassingly, it was all she dreamed about, too. Instead of being worried about how her life would progress as an orphan, she daydreamed about seeing Luke VonBrandt naked again.

His hands touching her. His mouth tasting her. His cock filling her.

It was enough to drive her positively batty, and she was balancing precariously on the edge of losing it already.

"But you do want to sleep with me."

He let out a long sigh. "More than anything. But, Kara, it needs to be when you want me. Not when you're trying to escape feeling." Leaning forward, his bright blue eyes caught and held her gaze. "I want you so much it hurts. But you weren't with me in there earlier. You were just going through the motions."

She frowned. He was right - again.

"Even so, there's something you aren't telling me."

He rubbed his face and looked away from her again. Definitely hiding something.

"I don't know if you noticed my mother's bond

marks."

"She has double bracelets, where I only have one." Kara had noticed and wondered at the significance. But everything about this family was so secretive. They'd lived in town for decades, maybe longer. They owned one of the biggest ranches outside of town, but didn't do anything with it. No cattle. A few horses. Mostly it was just forested land.

"When we complete the bond the second set of bracelets will appear."

"Complete, as in... oh." What was one more set of tattoos? That certainly wasn't a reason for him to run for the hills.

"It also means that we will complete the link between us and our emotions will be tied together." His words slowed as he reached the end of the sentence.

Emotions? "So if I'm sad, you'll be sad? God, how do you deal? I can feel physical stuff already, and the closer you are the stronger it gets."

"The emotional tie will work very similarly. You won't be forced into an emotion, but we will be able to read each other's. The closer we are in proximity, the stronger the signal, so-to-speak." He paused, and she met his gaze again.

"This is already exhausting. Sharing every physical pain. Did you feel my injuries after the accident? How did you move? I know I broke bones."

"It was nearly impossible for the first few hours. I can't remember how many times I stumbled flat on my face that night."

The idea that he'd felt every pain and injury she'd had from the accident was terrifying. To suddenly be incapacitated because of an injury someone else experienced... "Will it always be that way?" she asked.

"Yes. But, if and when we complete the bond, you can be taught to tune some of it out, so it's not constantly in your head."

That was good news. At least there would be a little relief, but not until they slept together. And if they did sleep together and completed the bond... what would happen if they ever broke up? How could you leave someone you could literally *feel*?

"Something else," she paused and watched him carefully. "Why were you and your brother naked in the woods that morning after the accident?"

His face flushed and he avoided her gaze.

"Is your family part of some cult or nudist group?"

"No, nothing like that," he answered. His blue eyes finally looked back up at hers, and she gasped. The irises were changing from sky blue to yellow gold. "My family is something more than human. It's why we have the bonding spell."

"More than human? Meaning what? What are you?"

"My father is descended from a long line of werewolves. The history of our pack stretches back to ancient Ireland."

A giggle slipped from between her lips, and she shook her head. He couldn't be serious. Werewolves? The magickal healing spell had been a stretch, but left with no other explanation, she'd had to go with it. But now he wanted her to believe he was descended from a pack of wolves.

"Prove it."

Luke stood and stared down at her, his gaze still bright and yellow. He started unbuttoning his shirt and she watched, mesmerized as muscle after muscle of his torso was revealed. Then he pulled the shirt off and she licked her lips --washboard abs, thick muscular arms, and broad shoulders. Damn he was beautiful.

Next went the pants and boxers. For a moment, he stood in all his glory. Then he got down on all fours, and she watched incredulously as bones shifted and his face changed. Fur sprouted all over his body and within the space of ten seconds, a large grey wolf stood in the middle of the kitchen instead of Luke.

"Oh my, God!" She stood, her chair clattered to the floor, and she backed toward the door that led into the back yard. Her heart raced inside her chest and breathing became difficult. She gasped for breath and fumbled behind her for the doorknob. Black spots invaded her vision, and the room started to spin.

A moment later she opened her eyes, surprised to find herself stretched out on the family sofa in the living room. The wolf was gone, and Luke sat on the coffee table, his hands clasped together and his lips stretched painfully tight. His eyes had shifted back to their natural bright blue and were watching her expectantly.

"I guess that explains why you and Noah were naked out in the woods together, huh?"

The tiniest flicker of amusement crossed his face before blanking again and he nodded. "This isn't something we tell people, Kara. You can't ever tell anyone."

That's why he looked like he'd swallowed a porcupine. He was worried she'd go and tell other people he and his brother could turn into wolves.

CHAPTER EIGHT

He shifted on the table uncomfortably and waited. She was still just staring, as if contemplating his fate. Had it been a mistake to show her? Would she betray him and his family? What if he'd singlehandedly ruined his entire family's life? The only comment she'd made so far was about him and Noah out in the woods on Thursday night.

"Even if I wanted to tell anyone, Luke, no one would believe me."

He narrowed his gaze and glared, meeting her blue eyes straight on. She was being much more levelheaded about this than he'd expected. No running and screaming for the hills. She *had* passed out, though.

"I'm not even sure I would believe me, except that I watched it happen." She sat up slowly and eyed him warily, like he might leap on her at any second.

"I won't hurt you, Kara."

"I believe you. It's just ... unsettling." She tucked her feet under her body and hugged one of the large throw pillows to her chest, creating a barrier of sorts between herself and him. "Do you recognize people when you are a..."

"A wolf?" he finished for her.

She nodded.

"Yes, I'm aware, in control, and can understand every word you say."

"Is everyone in your family able to change?"

He shook his head. "My mother is human. The enchantment passes down from my father."

Her breathing was even. Her heart wasn't racing anymore. She appeared calm. Hope soared in his chest. Maybe, just maybe, she wouldn't completely shut him out. He could dream. She was the only woman he'd ever wanted to share his secret with, and now that he had, he could only wait and hope she accepted him for what he was. Everything he was - wolf and man.

His dad had been lucky to find mom. She'd been raised in a supernatural-friendly home. Her mother – Luke's grandmother - was a witch, and knew more things about the world than anyone he'd ever met. His dad said Grandma Willows had known he was a werewolf the second he'd walked into their house. He'd never had to have this awkward conversation with mom. She'd grown up knowing about all the supernatural creatures that hid in plain sight among humans.

Finding out his dad - Aaron VonBrandt - was a werewolf hadn't even been a bump in the road for his mom.

It was different for him. Kara didn't grow up with any inkling that the world was anything more than what it appeared.

The death grip she had on the throw pillow loosened and she placed it to her side. "So... I..." She paused.

"You don't have to say anything," he answered, reaching for her knee. As his fingers brushed over her leg she flinched, and he cursed inwardly. She must find him repulsive. Some kind of freak. He was. Her rejection had haunted his dreams. Now it was happening for real. Jerking back his hand, he swallowed and looked down at the hardwood. "Sorry. I know I'm a freak of nature. I just -"

Her fingers touched his face and slid beneath his chin, lifting his head to meet her gaze. He didn't see fear or disgust in her soft cornflower blue eyes. Instead, he saw desire.

Life sparked in those beautiful eyes, and she leaned forward more, pressing her lips against his. She was purposeful, and he had no intention of stopping her this time. The wolf within him howled with pleasure as her sweet taste spread through his mouth.

Moving with the grace of the predator he was, he

lifted her from her seat on the couch and took her place, then placed her across his lap so that she straddled him. Her thighs squeezed on either side of his hips, and he slid his hands up her back beneath the loose t-shirt she wore. Her skin was so soft.

A sweet moan growled from her throat, and she moved her mouth to his cheek, then to his neck, putting her neck against his face. Inhaling deeply, he took in her sweet female scent mixed with vanilla body wash. Goddess in heaven, she smelled so good.

He licked her neck and then kissed the delicate skin tenderly, not wanting to leave a mark on her porcelain skin. A shiver fluttered through his body as she nipped at his ear, not taking the tender route with him. It was fine with him. She could bite and scratch all she wanted. He'd wear any mark she gave him proudly.

Their tongues danced against each other, both fighting to go deeper. Harder. More.

He tugged at her shirt, and she lifted her arms. One last tug pulled it over her head, and he feasted his gaze on her gorgeous breasts. Pink areoles and erect nipples were only inches from his mouth. He palmed one breast and pulled her closer, taking the other into his mouth. She threw back her head and arched her back, giving him even easier access.

Her body was heaven for him. He swirled his tongue around her nipple, teasing and delighting in the shivers and moans his attention elicited. Even a little nip was met with a gasp of pleasure.

She rocked her body up and down, rubbing her sex across the bulge at his crotch. His erection pressed uncomfortably against his pants, straining to be freed. Thoughts of feeling her warm sheath squeezing him filled his mind. She would be perfect. He knew she would.

But his gut told him that wasn't the next step. She wasn't ready for the emotional bond that would come with them having sex. It would overwhelm her. He had to hold back and give her more time to come to terms with her loss. Honestly, he wasn't sure he was ready either.

What he was sure of, was that he wanted to taste her. All of her.

He switched hands and moved his mouth to her other breast, rolling the nipple he'd already tasted between his thumb and forefinger, applying just enough pressure to keep it hard and erect. The tiny mewls and moans from Kara were driving him insane. He needed more of her. Now.

Scooting forward on the couch he slid both his hands behind her and gripped her shoulders, pulling her back.

"What's wrong?" Her gaze snapped to his. Damn she looked so beautiful. Her strawberry blond hair was a little mussed and her lips were swollen and pink from kissing. He pulled her closer and stole a quick kiss.

"Nothing's wrong. You amazing and I was planning to lay you out on the table and taste you a bit more."

"I ... I've never." Her eyes widened, and she bit the edge of her bottom lip. "I never let-"

"Will you let me?" He watched her contemplate his request for a moment before swiping his tongue over one of her pebbled nipples, reveling in the shiver that coursed across her body. "Please," he mumbled around her breast. "I want to taste every inch of your beautiful body."

"Okay."

It was barely a whisper, but he heard it loud and clear. Carefully, he laid her backward, resting her on the coffee table in front of him. He caught the hem of her yoga pants and pulled, taking the pants and panties together, leaving her completely exposed and bared to his gaze. She was so gorgeous. Her pussy was completely bare except for a small triangle of light hair on her mound. The swollen pink lips of her sex glistened, and the smell of her arousal made him even harder. Damn, it was going to be harder than he thought to keep himself in check.

Tossing her clothes aside, he pushed her legs up over his shoulders and knelt to the floor between her thighs. She was tense and holding her breath. He ran his hands up her flat stomach toward her breasts and kneaded them until he felt some of her tension fade and her breathing quicken.

His mouth was so close to her sex. He knew she could feel every breath. Her body trembled like a leaf. It gave him great pleasure to know he would be the very first to ever give her this.

He pulled his hands back and slid them beneath her ass, cupping it and pulling her forward and up to his mouth. She tensed again, and he trailed his mouth along the inside of one thigh toward her sweetness, kissing and nipping gently until she was purring like a kitten.

He pulled her close and plunged his tongue deep, curling it forward and dragging it slowly along her slit to the hard little nubbin peeking out from under a hood of pink flesh. She tasted like honey and woman. His dick twitched, and he took a deep breath, trying to reign in his excitement. This was for her. Just her.

A gasp rasped from her chest and she clenched her heels into his back, pushing herself against his exploring tongue. He smiled and hummed against her flesh, loving the cries of pleasure that followed. Her hands found their way to his hair, and he winced as she jerked against him and gripped his hair tightly.

He kneaded her ass with his fingers, lifting and dropping her just the slightest as he plunged his tongue in and out. The momentum gave him a little further reach. Her hips rolled and twisted away from his mouth.

"Oh, no, baby. You haven't felt the best part yet." He pushed her up the table and leaned against her thighs, opening her even further. Latching onto her clit with his mouth, he sucked the swollen nubbin into his mouth and held it while he put his hands back to work on her nipples. He tweaked and rolled them as he did the same with her clit, and she arched beneath him, a wail tearing from her throat.

He felt her soar into that place of bliss and dreamed of the moment when they would share a moment like this completely bonded. For now, he would enjoy her pleasure, thankful she'd allowed him to give her this moment. She writhed beneath his hold and whimpered as her body shuddered through wave after wave of an orgasm.

***

Goosebumps prickled across her body. The slight sheen of sweat that had accumulated was now cold under the fan of the living room.

Amazing.

That was the only word even close to describing what she'd just experienced.

Luke slipped an arm beneath her back and another beneath her legs, standing and lifting her in one movement. He cradled her against his chest like she was something precious. She could never be afraid of him. Even though the werewolf thing was a little unsettling, being something more than human wasn't what defined him as a person. As a man. As someone she could see herself falling in love with.

The feelings were there. It wasn't just a rebound from having her heart broken over Vincent. There was a deeper connection between Luke and herself, something more than she'd ever felt with Vincent. Maybe it was the bond Luke talked about. Even if it was, she liked it. Selfishly, it gave her something to cling to in a world that had ceased to have purpose.

She buried her face against his chest and listened to the steady *thump* of Luke's heart. He was her new constant.

They were moving through the house now. Her toes brushed the wall as he carried her down the hallway. He turned into her bedroom and set her gently in the center of her bed. Then pulled her comforter up to cover her shivering body.

Kara opened her eyes and gazed up at him in the dimming light filtering through the half-closed drapes. "Stay. Please."

He nodded, sinking to his knees on the floor next to her bed.

She grabbed the edge of her comforter and pulled it back, putting her naked form into his direct line of sight. She liked the little hitch in his breath and the way his eyes drank her in like she was the most beautiful thing he'd ever seen. She couldn't remember Vincent ever looking at her that way. How could she have let that go as long as she did?

Didn't matter now. It was over. She didn't want to ever think about or see Vincent Harris again.

Luke stripped down to his boxers and slid into the bed with her, drawing her into his arms and covering them both with her comforter. She drank in his spicy male scent and nuzzled his chest, settling into the comfortable crook of his shoulder. Sleep came easily to her contented body.

CHAPTER NINE

The trill of an alarm spurred her from a deep sleep. Her bed was unnaturally warm, and her leg was draped over... another leg. She popped her eyes open and pushed up. Luke's blue eyes stared up at her and a smile curved his lips.

"Morning." His deep voice dripped with affection and his scruffy face was sexy as hell. He reached over to the nightstand and tapped the face of the wailing phone. The annoying alarm stopped instantly.

"Morning," she answered.

A second later she was on her back, and he was leaning over her with a wolfish grin. He pressed a soft kiss to her lips and then another on each of her bare breasts, sucking on one nipple and then the other until they stood erect. His gaze traveled up from her breasts to her face again. "Your nipples were feeling a little neglected. I couldn't have that."

She snorted through a laugh.

His smile widened even further, and his blue eyes sparkled. He kissed her again, sweeping his tongue into her mouth and nibbling on her bottom lip.

Damn. Her core clenched, and moisture pooled between her legs. God, she wanted nothing more than his cock buried deep inside her. But then she remembered what came tethered to that choice, and decided she could wait a little longer. It wasn't going to be easy, though.

"It's good to hear you laugh, Kara. I'll have to be sure I say hello to your gorgeous breasts every morning."

She couldn't help it. A grin spread across her face and she laughed again.

"I can keep saying hello," he added. "There's more of you to say hi to." He dropped his head and began trailing his tongue down her stomach.

"No!" She grabbed his arms and twisted underneath him and tried to crawl to the edge of the bed. "I have to get dressed. I refuse to be late on the first day of school."

He moaned and flopped to the side, releasing her from the weight of his body. She scrambled off the bed and ducked into her bathroom. The cold tile made her shiver and wish she was back underneath Luke.

She started the shower and stood with just the tip of her fingers under the stream of water until it heated to a bearable level. Then she stepped in and sighed, closing the glass door. The hot water sluiced over her body, between her breasts, and down to her feet. The shower steamed up quickly, and she took a deep cleansing breath.

"Is there room for me in there?"

She squeaked, his presence in the bathroom taking her by surprise. "You can have the shower when I'm done," she protested, her voice slowing with each word. He'd stripped naked and had opened the shower door. Her gaze traversed up and down his lean muscular body and heat swirled inside hers. He was all muscle. All man. And very erect. *No! I can't do this. Not right now.*

"Are you going to invite me in?"

"Apparently you aren't a vampire and are going to do exactly as you please without my permission." She grabbed his arm and pulled him inside the shower, closing the door to capture what little steam was left. "Quit letting out the warm air."

His laughter echoed in the tiled shower. He hugged her from behind, his erection prodding her backside teasingly. His lips pressed to her neck and she let her head loll to the side, giving him better access. "I'm definitely not a vampire, but your neck is very tempting."

She pulled away in a start and whirled to face him. "Are vampires real, too?"

"Not that I know of." He fondled her breasts, and she leaned back, moaning low in her throat as the tension in her body slipped away. At least she didn't have to worry about vampires jumping out of the shadows at her. Just wolves.

He turned her around and claimed her mouth, plunging his tongue in and sweeping it against hers. She gripped his shoulders and pulled herself closer. It was as if their bodies had minds of their own. The thought of letting go of him was nearly unbearable. How was she ever going to get to school today?

"This shower is not progressing very productively," she said against his mouth. It didn't come out very clearly, but he got the gist.

"Sorry." He dropped his hands to his sides and took a step back.

The absence of his touch nearly brought tears to her eyes. But the choice had been discussed and decided. They weren't going to complete the bond... not yet. He'd said she wasn't ready. Maybe he wasn't ready either. Feeling each other's emotions sounded like a huge step. It probably was. She didn't really understand what was going on, but she did know she needed some space or she was going to go crazy. It was like she was on a drug that made her hornier than a sixteen-year-old boy.

She hurriedly washed and rinsed her hair and body, willing herself not to look at Luke. It was so hard. Even with her eyes closed she could feel his gaze on her. Her skin warmed, not from the water, and nerves tingled throughout her body.

"It's all yours." She stepped out of the shower and closed the glass door before he could speak.

Grabbing a towel from the rack on the wall, she tip toed out of the bathroom and pulled on the baggiest clothes she could find. An old pair of sweatpants and an oversized Taylor Swift t-shirt should do the trick. It might be the first day of school, but she needed to feel as unsexy as possible. She wound her wet hair up into a twisted bun and wrapped a few hairbands around it to keep it in place.

The water turned off in the bathroom and she scurried out of the bedroom, not trusting what she might do if she saw his bare skin again. It was all so overwhelming, and the idea that there was more to the bond, that it would get stronger, was starting to freak her out. There's no way she could live day in and day out like this.

***

Holy shit. What the hell am I going to do? Luke toweled off and poked his head out of the bathroom. Kara's room was empty. She'd already fled.

That's what she'd done. He'd seen the panic in her eyes when she got out of the shower. The bond was pulling at them both, and it had only gotten stronger after they slept next to each other last night. His parents said it would tug at each of their consciousness, but this was beyond a little tug. This was more like a magnetic field pulling them together until they couldn't help themselves any longer. They were an unfinished song. A half cooked meal.

A force of nature that would not be checked.

He had to give her space. Time to make this choice on her own.

After putting his suit back on from last night, he ventured out her bedroom door and saw her going through a stack of books on the kitchen table. Her gorgeous blonde hair was drawn back into a severe bun that looked painful, and her curves were expertly hidden by baggy pants and a t-shirt four times too large for her. The smallest bit of her shoulder peeked out from the neck of the shirt when she leaned to the side and his mouth watered.

Damn. This is bad.

"Kara." His voice sounded worse than a bullfrog's.

She squealed in surprise and whirled to face him. Her cheeks flushed red and he could hear her heartbeat racing. But it was her scent that nearly knocked him on his ass. He could smell her arousal as plainly as if they'd never left her bed. Honey-sweet and more tempting than anything he'd ever tasted in his whole life.

"You can't come in here." She gathered up an armful of books and shoved them into a backpack. "I don't know what is going on with my brain or my body. But I can't touch you or be near you for a while. Maybe in a few hours I'll be able to think straight."

He took a step forward and she raised her hand, motioning clearly for him to stop. His feet obeyed, but his mind didn't want to. "It's the bond." It was the only explanation he could offer her. He didn't think it would fade, though, even if they did avoid each other.

She threw the backpack over her shoulder and grabbed her purse from the seat of one of the kitchen chairs. "I'm going to class." She gave him a wide birth as she crossed the living room and disappeared out the front door.

He released the breath he hadn't realized he'd been holding and then walked into the kitchen. Pulling his cell phone from his pocket, he dialed his brother and waited.

"What's up?" Noah's voice growled on the other end of the line. "I don't do early classes. Why you calling me?"

"I need you to pick me up. I'd walk, but I'm wearing dress clothes. And I have a nine o'clock class." Luke rubbed his chin, scratching at the stubble. It was too hot in August to go much longer than a couple of days, but all his stuff was at the AKO house, and he hadn't been able to find any disposable razors in Kara's bathroom. Not that he'd really wanted to use her vanilla scented shaving cream on his face either. Noah would never have let him live that down.

"Okay, fine. I'll be there in a few." He heard the rustle of sheets and his brother extricating himself from them. "What about Kara? Does she want a ride to school?"

"No. She already left."

"Why didn't she bring you to campus?" Noah asked.

"She thinks we need space between us."

"I take it you explained what would happen if y'all got busy, huh?" Noah snorted through a laugh.

Luke growled. "I don't need this from you right now. Just get over here and pick me up."

"Fine. Fine. I'm coming."

CHAPTER TEN

Kara glanced up at the clock on the classroom wall. *8:29.* Time was moving slower than snail slime, and this first class was one of her core music theory classes. She needed to pay attention to Professor Hickson. She'd had him last year for Music Theory 101, and he was no joke. Her mind just wouldn't cooperate. Even her body refused to relax.

Instead, she could still feel Luke's lips on her neck; his hands on her breasts. Warmth pooled between her legs, and she squirmed in her chair, desperate for the class to end so she could disappear into her math class and hide at the top of the lecture hall. There were only thirty students in Music Theory 201. Nowhere to hide, and unless she was imagining it, they all seemed to be staring at her.

God! They were!

"Kara?" It was Professor Hickson's voice. "Kara, are

you okay?"

She snapped her gaze to the lanky middle-aged professor. His black-rimmed glasses sat low on his long nose and his grey eyes were narrow, but filled with concern. He was a nice man, but he didn't appreciate his students being inattentive.

"Sorry, Professor Hickson. I'm just not feeling well."

"Very well, but I don't want to see you in my class later today asking about the syllabus we just went over."

"No sir, of course not," she answered, shaking her head. She hadn't heard a word he'd said, but she'd get Amy or Trish to fill her in on what she missed while spaced out. She glanced at her friends sitting to her right. Both girls smiled encouragingly.

***

"You know, if you would just tell him what happened, Hickson would understand," Trish offered softly as they crossed campus from Treynor Arts Center to the BD Lewis Math Building.

"No, it's okay. I'd rather just keep it private. I don't need the whole department showing me pity all semester."

"Kara, there's nothing wrong with easing your way back into school. The teachers would understand," Amy added.

"We miss you at the house. You're not coming back, are you?" Trish asked, hooking her arm around Kara's.

"I'm sorry," she started, "I just can't. Not right now. With my parents and everything else, I just need some space."

"Everything else?" Amy stepped ahead and halted the trio's walk. "Would everything else have anything to do with that?" She turned and pointed across the lawn.

Kara followed Amy's hand until her gaze came to rest on Luke. He was leaning against a tree, arms folded across his broad chest, just staring.

"We didn't even get to talk to you at the funeral. The VonBrandt family had you surrounded like they were your personal bodyguards." Amy started walking along the sidewalk again and Kara followed silently.

Trish didn't say anything, but she could feel her friend's desire to know the answer to that very same question hanging in the air, just as thick as the August humidity right before a thunderstorm.

"Luke and I -"

"Are an item." Trish giggled. "Girl, we know that. You blush redder than a ripe tomato every time he looks at you."

"I still can't believe you dumped Vincent." Amy turned to face her. "You've been together forever. I thought you two were soul mates."

Kara scoffed. "Hadn't you heard? His dick is soul mates with half the campus. I can't believe he hid it from me as long as he did." She shuddered, wondering just how many women he'd slept with while they'd been together. Thank God they'd always used protection.

Her friends gasped at her blunt statement. But, whether they already knew why she and Vincent parted ways or not, they did an excellent job of making her believe it was news to them. She smiled. Amy and Trish were the reason she'd joined KAS last year. They were fun and great at rallying school spirit, but now after everything that had happened with her roommate and ex-boyfriend, she was ready to just stay at home.

Driving the ten minutes back and forth from campus to the house held a certain appeal. Private, quiet, and away from the prying eyes of the campus gossip mongers. Not that she could really escape that. If she and Luke really did become an item, the whole town would start talking about it. Everything the VonBrandt's did was scrutinized and gossiped about. They had a lot of money, and most of the campus considered Luke and Noah two of the most eligible bachelors on campus.

It didn't hurt that they were sexy as sin either.

"Earth to Kara," Trish teased. They reached the doors and had to part ways. Neither of her pals were taking classes in the BD Lewis Math Building during this period.

Kara smiled at Trish and waved her hand. "Gotta run. I'm fine. I'll see you girls at lunch, okay?"

They waved back and nodded.

***

Math class had been uneventful, except that the professor thought it would be nice to give a crap load of homework on the first day. Kara wandered out of the building and into the sweat-inducing, sweltering heat outside. Damn, it was hot. And it was only ten in the morning.

She had a free period before lunch. Might as well head to the Sub and wait for Trish and Amy to catch up. Turning, she took a few steps before freezing in place. Vincent was approaching, his gaze locked onto her. She glanced around quickly, but didn't see either of the VonBrandt brothers. *Shit.* She really didn't want to talk to his sorry-no-good-cheating-ass.

He waved and she frowned.

"Kara."

She tried to walk past him, but he blocked the sidewalk. So she just walked around him. He didn't get the hint and followed along beside her, heeling like a well-trained dog.

"I don't want to talk to you, Vincent. I don't want to see you." She glanced up at him for a second and grimaced. He had a black eye, cuts above both eye brows, a busted swollen bottom lip, and a swollen nose. *Dear God.* They had wailed on him good. She felt only the tiniest bit of sympathy for the obvious pain he must be in, but mostly she was glad. He'd used her and lied to her. She deserved better.

"Kara, baby -"

"Don't you dare 'baby' me!" She stopped and shoved him away. He was so close to her she could smell his familiar minty aftershave. It was a scent she used to enjoy, but now it made her want to gag. "You cheated on me with my *roommate*! And God knows how many other women from what I've heard."

"You can't listen to him."

"I. Saw. You." She shook her head and took a step away, only to be yanked backward by her arm. Pain shot through her shoulder.

"He just wants to get into your pants. He's always wanted you."

"Let me go." She twisted from his grasp and gasped, stumbling back as a large figure knocked Vincent to the ground.

It was Luke. And Vincent wasn't faring any better in this fight than the last. Luke straddled him, connecting his fists over and over with Vincent's face and ribs. She winced at the sickening sound of bone breaking and ran forward.

"Stop."

Luke's arm froze in midair. He rolled his neck and stood, stepping away from Vincent and pulling her close to his side. "Don't you ever touch her again." He leaned over and Vincent cringed away from him. "Do you understand me? She's mine."

Vincent nodded and scrambled to his feet. He took a couple steps away and then turned back.

She could feel Luke's arm tense under her hand.

"You'll be sorry, VonBrandt." With that threat he stormed off, pushing through the crowd of people that had gathered.

Kara shifted uneasily from one foot to another. Students had gathered when the fight started. Phones were out. Pictures had definitely been taken and probably videos would be all over social media within minutes.

Luke released a deep sigh, grabbed her hand and led her away from the crowd. By the time they reached the Sub, most of the onlookers had moved on.

She pulled him to the side, into an alcove just outside the entrance to the food court doors. "You shouldn't have done that. I was taking care of it."

"He hurt you, Kara." His blue eyes flashed with a fire of aggression she hadn't seen in him before. This primal side of him was more than a little overwhelming. But, as much as his machismo irritated her, she couldn't help but find it sexy too.

Damn her traitorous hormones. She couldn't even be upset with him without wanting to plaster herself against his solid body and beg him to kiss her. Her body wasn't playing fair.

She shook her head, clearing away her carnal thoughts. "I'm not yours. You don't get to say that. And you don't get to act like an animal because someone is a dick to me. I may be an emotional basket-case right now, but this," she waved her hands at him, "is not helping matters at all."

His eyes turned bright yellow for just a second and he snarled. Not a little rumble. A full blown animalistic growl thundered from his chest.

Her body quivered and liquid heat pooled at her core. His nostrils flared like he could smell her arousal. *Thank God we're in public.* If they'd been anywhere private she knew neither one of them would still be clothed.

He narrowed his gaze, staring like he was trying to intimidate her into agreeing that he'd done the right thing. But he hadn't. He'd be damn lucky if Vincent didn't press charges.

Kara stood her ground and glared. Luke didn't scare her. She knew no matter how angry he was, she would never be in danger from his hand.

"Fine," he said through gritted teeth. "If you want to deal with assholes by yourself - go right ahead."

"I will."

The veins in his neck pulsed visibly and a tic in his cheek twitched. He was wound just as tightly as she was. She just hoped Vincent was smart enough not to confront Luke again anytime soon. That idiot was a glutton for punishment, though, and she wouldn't put it past him to gather up a few of his pals and try to jump Luke when he wasn't expecting it.

She almost called after him. She wanted to tell him to watch for Vincent, but when she opened her mouth, words wouldn't come out. A frown pulled at the corners of her mouth and she ground her teeth. Hopefully the incident would blow over. But she wasn't betting on it.

CHAPTER ELEVEN

It was after five when she pulled into the lot next to Everyday Joe's. She hadn't seen or heard from Luke since the altercation this morning. Slamming the door on her jeep, she stalked across the parking lot toward the front entrance of the country western bar. She needed something. Anything to get her mind off stripping Luke VonBrandt naked. Even as mad at him as she was, she couldn't stop thinking about touching, tasting, and having every inch of him all to herself.

"Aaargh!" she growled under her breath and pulled open the door. A wave of cool air conditioning washed over her damp neck, instantly making her forget the sweltering August heat outside.

The scent of grilling beef assailed her nostrils, and she smiled. She was starving. Lunch had not appealed to her stomach, and she'd spent her entire lunch hour listening to Amy and Trish cackle on about the fight between Luke and Vincent. It hadn't surprised her. She'd known the whole campus would be gossiping in a matter of minutes.

She headed for the bar, passing by a small crowd gathered in the karaoke corner. Some poor soul was wailing on a song like she was the next Kelly Clarkson, except she wasn't even on key. Kara winced as the girl went for the last note of the song and failed miserably.

Sliding into a seat, she propped her chin on her elbows and waited for Joe. He was chatting with a couple at the opposite end of the bar. She didn't feel like company and had claimed the very last stool closest to the far wall. Hopefully the newly arrived college crowd would keep their distance.

"How was the first day?"

First day of school? Or first day officially as an orphan? She closed her eyes and took a deep breath. "It's been a hell of a day."

His eyebrows raised. "You can't drink here, baby girl, sorry."

"I know, Joe. I just needed ... I wanted ..." Why had she come here? Why hadn't she just gone home? "Can you just pour me a coke?"

"Of course, hon." He stepped away for a moment, filled a glass, and then returned, setting a full glass in front of her.

"Wanna tell me what's going on with you and Luke VonBrandt?"

She took a sip of the sweet carbonated beverage and then sighed as it burned its way down her throat. "You saw the video, didn't you?"

He nodded.

"It's complicated, Joe."

"Your new ink tells me that, baby girl," he said, leaning down.

She swallowed and met his gaze head on. "What do you know about my tattoos?"

"Enough to know that you're in deep with that family. How much do you know?"

"A lot."

"Good."

She waited for more. For questions, but they didn't come.

Instead he just nodded his head and laid his large hand over her small one in a comforting gesture. "People are starting to notice you're here. You should get home, unless you want to be grilled about this morning's events."

"Yeah," she said, glancing around the half-empty bar. It was slow, even for a Monday night, but he was right, people were starting to stare. It was the curse of small town life. Everyone did their best to know everyone else's shit. "I'll see you later."

"No problem. I'm gonna give Holly your shifts this

week. Let me know if you plan to take off next week too, okay?"

"I will. Thanks, Joe." She slid from the stool and wove her way through the tables to the front door.

Halfway to her car, her purse started buzzing. She pulled it out, and her heart leapt in her chest. The Somewhere Sheriff's Dept ID flashed on the glass screen.

"Hello?" Her voice sounded like she'd swallowed a toad.

"Miss McClure? Kara?" It was Randall West, one of her dad's best friends and Somewhere's Sheriff. As a lawyer, her dad knew most of the officers in Somewhere, but Randall and his wife Tracy were always coming over for dinner and a game of poker.

"Is something wrong, Mr. West? I mean, Sheriff? Sorry." She swallowed, hoping the knot forming in her stomach would not get worse.

"It's okay, Kara. We've known each other long enough to make that confusing. But, I need to ask you to come down to the station if you can. We have Luke VonBrandt in custody on aggravated assault."

"Vincent just had to go make it worse," she hissed. "Is he still there?"

"Kara, I need you to come down and give a statement."

Ignoring the repeated request, she continued. "Is

Luke okay?" Visions of him tearing up the sheriff's department office flashed through her mind. Surely he wouldn't, though. He was smarter than that... but Vincent was good at pushing buttons. If anyone could get someone to do something without thinking, it was Vincent Harris.

"Luke is fine. He refused to say anything." Randall chuckled. "It's driving Harris crazy. Still, I would really like to know what is going on, and I know Harris is only telling me half the story. He says he was just trying to talk to you when VonBrandt jumped him unprovoked."

"I'll be right there." Kara tossed her phone back into her purse and climbed into her jeep. She pulled out of the parking lot and was in front of the police station in less than five minutes.

Parking in the lot next to the small sheriff's office, she threw her vehicle into park and practically jogged from her jeep to the front of the building. She yanked open the door and walked past Edna at the front desk straight to Sheriff West's desk in the back.

"Kara McClure," Edna called. "Where do you think you are going?"

"Where are they?"

"Did Randall call you?"

"Edna! Where are they?"

The older receptionist pointed down the hallway.

Kara turned and stomped through the otherwise empty office to the interview rooms in the back. There were only three rooms in the back, and one of them was a file room.

One of the doors in the hallway opened, and Sheriff West poked his head out. "I thought I heard you." He beckoned her toward him and moved out of the doorway so she could enter the small bare room.

She nodded to him and turned, expecting to see Luke. Her blood boiled when Vincent's loathsome look met her gaze instead. His face looked worse than it had this morning, but she had no sympathy left for him. "You son of a turd eating hound dog!" Her voice rose in volume. "You drop the charges against Luke or I'll press the same ones against you. Or did you forget how you half wrenched my arm from its socket this morning?"

His blue eyes darkened hatefully and he shifted his gaze from her to the Sheriff and then back.

"Don't look at me, son. You're the one that said you were only trying to *talk* to Kara. This isn't the first time you've pissed off someone and gotten punched in the face for it."

"Fine." Vincent said, running his hands through his hair. He shot her a black look. "Have it your way, bitch. You aren't worth fighting over, anyway. If he wants my scraps, he can have them."

Heat flamed in her cheeks and tears clouded her

vision.

A crash came from behind a closed door on the other side of the hallway. She could hear Luke cursing on the other side.

"Vincent Lee Harris, your mother would be ashamed of you," the Sheriff growled.

Kara backed out of the room. She couldn't look West or Vincent in the eye. She just kept staring at the floor. How could he say those things? He'd cheated on her, yes, and now he acted like he'd never cared about her at all.

"Kara, I'm so sorry." West closed the door. "Should I book Vincent? What do you want to do? You said he hurt you?"

She shook her head. Her arm didn't even hurt anymore. It was just the only thing she could think of to use against Vincent. His parents would shit bricks if their perfect son got booked for assaulting a girl. His ex-girlfriend, to make matters worse.

Something hit the wall with a thud inside the room where Luke was, and she jumped, startled. Another volley of curses followed the crash.

"I just need to go home. I don't want to talk to either one of them." She turned and darted down the hallway, past Edna, out into the parking lot. Tears spilled from her eyes, burning salty trails down her cheeks.

She wiped her face and sucked in a deep breath. Climbing into her jeep, she shoved the stick into drive and pulled out of the lot. The drive to her house was short. Minutes later she pulled into the garage, parked, and pressed the button to close the metal door on the setting sun. It fell into place with a thud, and she entered the house.

Throwing her purse on the kitchen counter, she went straight for her dad's liquor cabinet and pulled out a bottle of whiskey. A shot or two of Maker's Mark would help her forget the shit of the day. The frustrations and the longings.

She downed two shots when the doorbell echoed through the house, breaking the dark silence with its cheerful tune. *Fuck. Now what?*

Leaving the empty shot glass on the counter, she walked through the kitchen to the front door. She stopped in front of it, holding her breath. It was him. She could feel him.

"Kara." Luke's deep voice bellowed from the other side of the door. "I know you're there."

"Go away," she said, but her voice was barely above a whisper.

"Please." His voice was raw, and she could almost feel his need through the closed door. Her body hummed with anticipation, begging her to let him inside.

She took the last step forward and opened the heavy front door.

Luke burst through, catching her into his arms and

capturing her mouth with his in one fluid movement. He kicked the door shut behind him and she heard him fiddle with the deadbolt until it fell into place.

He thrust his tongue deep into her mouth and his hands tore at the baggy t-shirt she was wearing. She lifted her arms, and he groaned his appreciation. He grabbed the hem of her shirt and pulled it over her head, releasing her mouth just long enough for the fabric to pass between them.

He pulled his head back and grasped her chin with one of his hands. She met his heated blue gaze and her insides melted. "I need you, Kara. I need you to be mine."

"I am." She was. It'd happened so fast, but she was his. Body and soul. She needed him with the same all-consuming desire that flowed from him.

He lifted her from the ground and carried her to her room, laying her on her back in the center of her bed. His hands caressed her breasts and deftly unhooked the front clasp of her bra, freeing them from their silk prison. Butterflies fluttered in her stomach as he ran his fingers down her torso and hooked them in the waistband of her sweats. Pulling slowly, he bared her completely and tossed the clothes over his shoulder. Then he stood and stripped out of his clothes.

Kara pulled her arms out of her bra and tossed it over the side of her bed just as he knelt between her legs. She caressed his arms as he settled his weight into the cradle of her hips, his hard erection prodding at her slick entrance.

His mouth sought hers again, and she moaned as his tongue danced with hers, mirroring what she hoped his cock would be doing inside her soon. She arched her hips and ran her hands down his muscled torso. God help her, his body was amazing.

CHAPTER TWELVE

Luke nudged her thighs open further and slid deep into her slick entrance. Her body welcomed him without hesitation, and her legs closed around his waist, pulling him even deeper. Supporting most of his weight on either elbow, he started to move in and out, slowly and methodically. She made sexy little sounds as he pulled almost all the way out before driving back in hard and deep.

His cock strained, and it took all his concentration not to come right away. He kept his movement varied and teasing, enjoying the feel of her nails raking up and down his back. Capturing a nipple with his mouth, he sucked hard, then scraped it with his teeth just a little. She moaned beneath him and arced her back, pushing the breast closer. Moving to the other nipple, he teased and laved until it too stood erect and hardened. A little nip brought a mewl of pleasure from her throat and tightened his balls.

He slipped his hands beneath her lower back, holding her in place and rolled so that she was straddling him. Her gorgeous breasts swung freely, enticing him with each movement. Her pink nipples were swollen and begging to be kissed. He pulled her closer so he could do just that, and her gaze heated, watching him from beneath hooded eyelids.

She tasted deliciously female. Soft, supple, and just a little sweet.

He grabbed her hips and guided her up and down on his dick, groaning as pleasure coursed through his body. A few moments into the ride, she took control. Placing her hands on his chest she rode him hard, grinding her mound against his pelvis and squeezing his dick for everything it was worth.

He sucked in a breath and reached for her bouncing breasts. Kneading them gently, he fondled until they swelled and hung heavy with arousal.

The sounds coming from Kara were exquisite - mewls and cries and moans meant to bring a man to the brink of losing control. He was so close, but unwilling to let it end just yet. Not that either of them would get much sleep tonight.

"You're so beautiful, Kara," he said.

Her legs tightened around his waist, and she breathed deeply. She was so close to orgasm, she was having trouble focusing on anything else.

He smiled, knowing exactly how he wanted her to finish.

Sitting up, he grasped her face and pulled her in close for a kiss. Their lips and tongues tangled and he swore she even nipped. Her hands gripped his shoulders, and she never quit moving, thrusting her body up and down his hard dick.

Moonlight flowed in through the cracks in the blinds and made her creamy skin glow. She was a glorious vision he didn't think he'd ever forget.

"L-Luke, please," she moaned, laying her head against his shoulder. "I need." Her body shuddered against his and she clung to him as if she were holding on for dear life.

He leaned her backward, wrapping one arm around her back and clamping his hand on her shoulder to hold her still. He could also balance on the one arm he had under her while he slipped the other hand between their sweat-slicked bodies. Tracing his fingers down her flat stomach, he slid it further down until he found her slick little bud.

Speeding up his thrusts, he teased her clit and whispered in her ear how good she felt and how hard he wanted to make her come. Her breathing had turned to pants by now and she moaned even more in response to his words.

"I want you to fly for me, baby," he said, nipping her

ear, and then pinched her clit. The only way this joining would satisfy the bond and seal them together permanently was through a mate lock. He hadn't known how to explain it ahead of time, and now he could only hope she wouldn't freak out.

He thrust hard, joining them deeply and completely. Her body shattered beneath him and a scream of pleasure tore from her lungs as an orgasm claimed her body. She was so tight, almost on the edge of painful. It was unlike anything he'd ever experienced with another woman. Then his body tensed and his shout joined hers as his seed poured into her and his dick swelled even more as her body squeezed harder.

She whimpered beneath him.

"It's okay, baby, just breath." He could feel her discomfort through their newly developing emotional link. She was concerned, but not frightened. He wasn't even really sure how long the lock would last, having been told it varied from person to person.

Dipping his head, he kissed the tops of her breasts and then slowly worked his way up her neck to her mouth, sending reassuring calming thoughts to her. It worked. She'd relaxed in his arms and returned the languid kisses, smiling against his mouth.

A few moments later the lock loosened. He slid from her body, rolled to her side, and sighed. "Goddess, you were amazing."

Her body shivered next to him and a small chuckle rolled from her chest. "I was, wasn't I. But, it was like I could feel your release alongside mine."

He rolled to his side and caught her gaze in the moonlight. Her blue eyes twinkled with amusement. Heat from their union still radiated from both their bodies, warming the air around them. He sighed, tracing a finger along the curve of her heaving chest. Her breathing was heavy and labored, like she'd just run a marathon.

"You did." He leaned and kissed her lips, running his tongue along the seam of hers. "And I felt yours."

"What happened with the...?"

He knew what she was referring to without asking. "It was a mate lock. The first time a bonded pair find release together they are locked together with magick while the bond seals in place."

"That sounded rehearsed," she answered, a giggle shaking her chest. "I would've loved to be a fly on the wall when someone made you memorize that line."

He chuckled, feeling her amusement. It'd been the most uncomfortable ten minutes with both of his parents he could remember in his entire life. "Yeah, it wasn't one of my favorite parent-son moments."

He stared at her, and waited. She had something she wanted to tell him.

"So, I am on birth control, just in case you were wondering." She rolled to her side and met his gaze.

Shit! He hadn't even thought to ask. "I ... I didn't. Kara, I should've asked. I'm sorry. But, the bond wouldn't have worked with a condom."

"Yeah," she paused, cocking her head to the side like a confused puppy dog. "I can feel your regret ... Can I just say, this is really strange."

He sighed. At least she wasn't pissed. "At least now we won't be quivering masses of upended hormones bent on stripping each other naked at every turn."

A smile curved her lips, and a second later he could feel her arousal and her excitement.

"Such a needy girl, you are." He grinned down at her.

Embarrassment bloomed in her mind and he shook his head. "Don't be embarrassed. I want more of you too."

"I'm not sure I'm going to handle this emotional sharing very well. It's a lot."

Her worry crept into his heart and he nodded. "My parents said they can teach us to control it. That we can learn to turn it off and on."

Relief flooded through her system and he relaxed, too. She was right. The emotional toil of this connection would wreak havoc on any sane person. He caught one of her hands and held it up into a beam of moonlight.

"What do you think of your new tats?"

***

She twisted her wrist and studied the second line of tattoos. They were nearly identical to the first bracelet, but now there were several places where they intertwined. It mirrored the way her heart was starting to feel, connected to Luke's. A warm wave of affection poured over her, and she looked up at Luke, meeting his gaze. His blue eyes shone like gemstones in the moonlight. She could feel everything. His concern, his possessiveness, his absolute adoration and... love.

He loved her. The words had not been spoken, but his feelings wrapped around her like a soft blanket. Tears pooled in her eyes, and she buried her face in his chest. It was so much. She didn't really know how she felt about him yet. She was attracted to him. He felt right. Safe.

A week ago she'd thought she was in love with Vincent, but the more she analyzed that relationship the more she knew she'd been fooling herself a long time. Still, where did that leave her with Luke? He'd opened her eyes to a whole new world beyond what she'd ever known existed. He'd saved her life, but in so doing had changed it completely without her permission. It was scary to think about all the things out in the world that might really exist. If werewolves did, who knew what else was out there?

"Kara?"

"I'm fine," she murmured against his skin.

"You forget the bond goes both ways and I just got body slammed by a tsunami of mixed emotions." He caressed her hair and stretched out on the bed, pulling her into the crook of his arm.

She sighed and snuggled as close to his warm body as she could. "Sorry. There's a lot on my mind."

"I'm here if you want to talk about it."

"Not right now." His spicy scent filled her lungs and she tried to ignore the arousal sparking inside her again. Sleep was what she needed, not another romp in the sheets. No matter how utterly fantastic that romp might be. Her body needed at least a *short* break.

He gave her a squeeze and stole a quick kiss.

She smiled. This was exactly where she needed to be for right now. Of that she was certain.

CHAPTER THIRTEEN

"Where do you want these boxes?" Noah hefted a large cardboard box from the back of his pickup. His face barely showed over the top.

"With the rest is fine. I'll sort through them later. Thanks." She pointed to the stack in the corner.

Luke came out of the house into the garage. Noah waved to his brother and walked to the back of Luke's blue pickup to grab another box. His black truck was parked a few yards away and had already been unloaded.

She'd been shocked how quickly they'd had all her things packed and cleared out of her room at the KAS house. Everything had been carefully stacked and secured into the back of their pickup trucks, and now it was almost all unloaded into the garage and house. Luke had made sure all her boxes of clothes and shoes were put in her bedroom so she wouldn't have to drag them in from the garage.

They'd packed everything without her, so Luke knew what was in all the boxes. After what happened with Samantha and Vincent, she just couldn't go back to the sorority, not even to pack, with her parent's house --her house-- sitting empty in town. Moving back home just seemed like the right thing to do.

She stood in the opening of the garage, watching the two guys go back and forth. She'd tried to help a couple of times, but neither one of them would hear of it and made her stand uselessly to the side and watch. It was sweet, but strange. She was an only child and used to doing everything herself.

Now she had Luke, his brother, their parents, and their aunts and uncles all checking in on her and asking if she needed something.

The first week of school had flown by. Classes were getting easier. She still cried anytime something reminded her of her parents, but it wasn't as overwhelming as it had been seven days ago.

It also helped to have Luke nearby. Their bond had been a source of strength for her. The empathic part had been difficult at first, but his mom and dad had shown them a few tricks to keep it from being overwhelming. Each day got more manageable, and now they were able to control when their emotions were shared.

She straightened and walked forward from the garage. Tonya and Aaron VonBrandt pulled up next to their son's truck. They were driving a white Avalanche. Kara laughed. This family was a fan of oversized vehicles. She glanced over at her small black Camry in the driveway. It looked so tiny compared to the VonBrandt's entourage.

Luke and Noah hurried over to their parents and grabbed the large takeout sacks from them. Tonya waved and smiled as they walked up the sidewalk toward her.

Luke made it to her first and leaned in to give her a kiss on the lips. "They brought lunch." He smelled as delicious as the food they'd brought from The Boiler Room in town square. She couldn't wait until they were alone again so she could taste him from head to foot.

His eyes widened and a grin spread across his face as she pushed her arousal through their bond. She giggled when his surged back to meet hers and made her tingle all over. Being able to turn each other on with merely a thought was definitely a perk of the empathic bond.

"Y'all quit making googoo eyes at each other and let's eat," Noah said, a chuckle shaking his chest. He passed them with two more bags from the restaurant.

"How many people do your parents plan to feed?" She glanced at Luke.

"Uncle Jason and Aunt Alyssa are coming over, too, with Logan and Evan."

"So your family just kinda shows up wherever? Without an invitation?"

He shrugged his shoulders and grinned. "Welcome to the pack. You're more than welcome to pop in to their houses unannounced as well. Just bring food. It's kinda the custom. We always bring food everywhere we go."

She smiled inwardly and turned to follow him through the garage and into the house. They did seem to bring food. And a lot of it. The BBQ Noah brought over last weekend before the funeral could've fed her for the entire week. But since Luke had practically spent every waking hour with her since Monday night, it'd only lasted two days. He ate more food at one meal than she ate in an entire day.

Tonya and Aaron filed in right behind them. "Did the boys get all your things safely back to the house?" His mother asked as they entered the kitchen.

"Yes." She nodded and started to get a stack of plates from the cabinet. "Thank you for bringing food, but you really don't have to."

Luke shook his head and frowned.

"But it does smell good," she added.

Tonya gave her a quick hug. "I'm glad. I'll set it out on the table and then the guys can dig in. I swear I can already hear my husband's stomach rumbling."

Kara pulled out a handful of silverware and set it on the counter. The doorbell chimed and she moved to go answer it, but Noah waved her off and disappeared around the corner.

Luke came up behind her and nuzzled her neck, and his breath ruffled through her hair.

She smiled and leaned back against his broad chest. "What are you doing? Your parents are right there," she whispered, smiling when his mom looked her way.

"I'm not doing anything bad," he growled, nipping at her ear.

That tiny touch sent a shiver down her spine. Food was the last thing on her mind. She was thinking about his hands running up and down her skin. How good it felt last time he'd tasted every inch ... *wait!*

"Stop," she squeaked, slithering from his grasp and pushing away the emotions he was shoving her direction. "You sneaky little..." Kara grabbed a plate from the counter and shoved it at his chest.

A wolfish grin split his face from ear to ear, and he gingerly accepted the plate, ducking away from her hand as she tried to come back and hit his arm. "Just having a little fun while you were relaxed. It's good to see you smile and laugh."

Their conversation was interrupted by laughter in the living room and what sounded like an invasion. Poking her head around the corner she waved at the new arrivals.

She recognized Jason VonBrandt, Luke's uncle. He'd helped get all her parents' paperwork in order, set her up on how to take care of the property she owned, and promised to help her out with any other financial advising. The small woman next to him must be his wife, Alyssa. He'd mentioned her and his two sons, but she'd not met them yet. The two teenage boys fist bumping Noah at the door looked just like Jason and she assumed they must be his boys.

It was nice to have the house full of people. Laughter and smiles were what should fill a house, not silence and sorrow. Her parents would be happy she'd found such good people to take care of her, even if they were a little supernatural. Not all of them were, though. Both of the women were human like her, bound to a VonBrandt through the magick.

Alyssa wore a half-dozen metal bangles on both wrists, but Kara could still see bits and pieces of her tattoo bracelets. She'd already seen Tonya's. Each woman's was a little different, but all held a Celtic quality to them - beautiful, intricate, and knotted together.

She wondered exactly how she was starting to feel about her developing relationship with Luke. With each passing day she felt more and more connected to him. Knotted together, just like the tattoos on both their wrists.

She leaned against the wall of the living room and watched his family laugh and pass around the plates of food. Luke looked up from across the room and smiled at her before turning back to his cousin.

A moment later he appeared by her side. She hadn't

even seen him move.

"Hungry? I made you a plate." Luke held out the plate and nodded toward it.

She accepted the offering of sliced prime rib, diced rosemary potatoes, and grilled asparagus. It smelled heavenly. She'd only eaten at The Boiler Room a few times, usually for her mom's birthday when Dad wanted to splurge. Her mom had been a great cook, and they rarely went out to eat.

"Thanks."

He winked and leaned against the wall next to her while she took a quick bite off one of the asparagus stalks. "Couldn't leave you over here alone without food. I know my family can be loud and overwhelming. They practically take over wherever they are."

She chuckled. "No kidding. They're stubborn too. In fact, I would go so far as to say that the word "no" does not exist in their vocabulary."

Laughter rolled up from his chest. He leaned over and kissed her temple. "You have only seen the tip of the iceberg."

She grinned up at him, losing herself in his bright blue eyes. He was so handsome, sweet ... passionate. Warmth crept up into her cheeks and his eyes twinkled in response.

Kara slipped her hand into her front jean pocket, snagging the spare house key she'd tucked there earlier.

"I have something for you." She pulled it out and held it up. "I'd like you to have this."

"A key to the house?" he asked, his voice low and filled with surprise. "Are you sure?"

She nodded, setting her plate on the end table next to her leg. "I know it's really fast. If you don't want it I-"

He snatched the key from her hand, cupped her face in his hands, and captured her mouth with his. The kiss was filled with hunger, but she could feel his love and adoration of her cascading in waves from their bond.

He kissed along her jaw and nibbled on her earlobe before whispering. "I love you, Kara. I've always loved you."

"I love you, too, Luke. More and more each day." She drank in his scent and wrapped her hands around his strong arms.

He kissed her again and then pulled back to meet her gaze. "Mine forever."

Her vision was blurry, but she could see the love in his gaze —feel it pouring out of him. "Forever."

I hope you enjoyed TO SAVE A MATE!

Please be sure to check out the other books in SOMEWHERE, TX Volume 1.

THE ROCKSTAR COWBOY by KC Klein
SADDLE UP by Jodi Vaughn
FIRE AWAY by R.L. Syme
WONDER LUST by Lavender Daye

Thank you for spending time with me in my world. I hope you will continue to visit.

XOXO

Krystal Shannan

Recommend it. Please help other readers find this book by recommending it to friends, readers' groups and discussion boards.

Review it. Please tell other readers why you liked this book by reviewing it at Amazon or GoodReads. If you do write a review, please send me an email at krystalshannan@yahoo.com so I can thank you personally. I always have a treat set aside for fans.

ABOUT THE AUTHOR

You Can Find Out More @ www.krystalshannan.com

Krystal Shannan goes to sleep every night dreaming of mythical realms with werewolves, vampires, fae, and dragons. Occasional a fabulous, completely human story slips into the mix, but powers and abilities usually crop up without fail, twisting reality into whatever her mind can conceive.

As a child, her parents encouraged her interests in Ancient Greek and Roman mythology and all things historical and magickal. As an adult, the interests only grew. She is a child of Neverland and refuses to ever stop believing in fairies. She is guilty of indulging in and being a Buffy the Vampire Slayer groupie as well as an Angel fan. For those of you unfamiliar with the world of Joss Whedon, you are missing out!

She also makes sure to watch as many action and adventure movies as possible. The more exciting the better. Yippee-Ki-Yay..... If you don't know the end of that phrase, then you probably don't like the same movies.

She enjoys reading romance in all genres, but especially paranormal. Her favorite book is ACHERON by Sherrilyn Kenyon. But really, if it has a 'Happily Ever After', she's on board!

Krystal writes stories full of action, snark, magick, and heartfelt emotion. If you are looking for leisurely-paced sweet romance, her books are probably not for you. However, for those looking for a magickal ride, filled with adventure, passion, and just a hint of humor. Welcome home.

Other Books By Krystal Shannan

Vegas Mates Series
Chasing Sam
Saving Margaret
Waking Sarah
Taking Nicole
Unwrapping Tess

Sanctuary, Texas
My Viking Vampire
My Dragon Masters
My Eternal Soldier (Spring 2015)

Somewhere, TX
To Save A Mate

Pool of Souls
Open House
Finding Hope

MacLaughlin Family
Trevor
Caiden
Harvey
Lizzy

Printed in Great Britain
by Amazon